The Great Portal Wars Trilogy
Book 1

The Worlds of Earth

Pauline Marquez

Revised Edition:
July 2015
All content by author Pauline Marquez
Edited by Laurie Larsen
Cover Art by Rick Cortez
Formatting by Polgarus Studios
Published in the United States of America

ISBN: 978-1-9909787-3-2 (Print)
ISBN: 978-1-9909787-1-8 (ePub)
ISBN: 978-1-9909787-0-1 (Kindle)

ACKNOWLEDGMENTS

This book has been many years in the making. Enough thanks cannot go out to all those who have helped me along in this journey. There have been many trials in my life between the first book and this third revision. I thank the Lord for my parents, Tony and Nancy Miosi, for being there every step of the way and helped me through very hard pressed times. To Sandy and Lou Marquez, thank you for your unconditional love. You will always be precious to me and I love you.

I want to thank my sister, Lisa Miosi, for her direction and marketing strategy with the first book. You always seem to have just the right connections at just the right time. I know we will continue to be a great team in the future! Next, I want to thank Emilie McDowell for her website creation and help. I would not be where I am today without her steadfast commitment.

Though this is the third revision, I cannot go without continuing to give credit for the tremendous amount of time and hours it took for the editorial work of the first revision of this book. Patricia Dimaio Simon taught me more than what I have room on this page to express. Her faithful dedication to this project will never be forgotten and I am truly grateful. In addition, I must give credit and special thanks to the editor's assistant, I owe more than I could ever repay to you as well. That credit goes to Patricia Miosi West. She stood by the editor's side until the job was done. This third revision was done by best-selling author, Laurie Larsen. Thank you so much Laurie for the work you did to fine tune this book! I am so thankful for you!

Though there are no pictures in this revision, to Nicole Rivera, Mika Rivera, Maria Forney, and Jon Proctor, I give you my many thanks for all the great artwork you did in the first revision to bring the book to life. Your hard work in bringing scenes to life will not be forgotten!

I want to also give special thanks to Rick Cortez for taking our vision for the book cover and bringing it to life with his brilliant graphic design work.

Within the pages of this book is a desperate fight for hope and the importance of never giving up. We all struggle with many trials through life. All of them are different, but all of them so very real. If you need a good book that deals with a battle to cling on to hope no matter what happens, then this trilogy is for you. Do not ever give up.

To my dear children, Emanuel, Rebekah, and Gabriel, you are my inspiration. I dedicate this book to you — my three darlings.

Contents

Chapter 1
The Wretched Daze

The horizon, once again, was painted. Its prismatic presence set fire to the early evening sky, then slowly dissipated, its colors growing weaker with every passing second. Darkness, knowing its time had come, followed the fleeing sun. The noises of the forest suddenly deadened. A deep stillness crept in as night drew its shade. Without cause or warning, a celestial wind, foreign to this world, arrived from deep inside the forest. The wind picked up in intensity as it began its search. The branches of the giant oak, maple and elm trees swayed in the direction of the winds' desire.

Outside this dense and forsaken forest stood a fifteen-year-old girl, wondering why she was there, yet completely powerless to run from this hidden magic. The celestial wind blew out of the forest, passing the one it sought. Then, it abruptly turned around and began to push against the girl's back. Her golden-brown hair blew uncontrollably in her face as the wind directed her into the forest. She found herself standing in front of a barely visible path, overgrown by weeds and thickets, and long since forgotten as it twisted its way along the forest floor. Her forehead crinkled in bewilderment.

"Jen, you must find me," the wind beckoned.

"Why are you calling me?" she whispered under her breath. "Why do you keep taunting me over and over again?"

Jen's life had turned into chaos when her father mysteriously disappeared a few short months ago. The magic of the forest ignored her pleas as it slowly and methodically tried to pull her in, but Jen shook her head and stood her ground. The longer she stood, the angrier she became. Muscles tightened, fists clenched, she screamed. The wind retaliated, this time blowing against her face, whispering her name again and again. She stood there, listening in fear and anger until, unable to take it any longer, she yelled, "Stop it! Stop it! Leave me alone. Don't call me here again!"

....

"Don't call me here again!"

"Jen, excuse me, Jen!" snapped Miss Pine, Jen's history teacher. The rest of the class broke out in laughter as Jen was jarred from yet another daydream.

"That's enough, class." After a moment, they settled down, and Miss Pine continued with the lesson, turning her back to the class and writing away on the whiteboard. The eyes of her classmates bore down on Jen. Living in humiliation had become the new norm for Jen. She had been rejected, and understood what it meant to be seen as a nobody.

A paper ball landed on her desk. She looked over and saw Jacob's dimpled-covered face, half-smiling. He gestured to it with his head, asking her to open it. Reluctantly, she did.

Unanimous vote from the class that Jen is the number one LOSER in the school! Congrats!

She calmly rolled it back up into a ball and threw it at his face, causing the classmates to chuckle.

Miss Pine didn't bother to turn around. "There will be a quiz on what I just said tomorrow and I won't be writing it on the board either," which left the class in a hiss of disgusted sighs.

As if things aren't bad enough, Jen thought, *there's nothing better than the feeling of being thrown out with the trash and completely forgotten.*

The thoughts about the dream danced around in her mind again. It was just a senseless dream, but at the same time, she never was willing to let it go. When it came, she both hated it and loved it. In a strange way, she clung to it as if it was all she had left of her father.

Jen broke that thought and stared at the whiteboard that was surrounded by a stained white wall, making sure to look as if she were paying attention. Then she let her mind drift back to happier times. She remembered her father's smile when she crossed the finish line first in the last cross-country meet he was at. How she missed that smile, that wonderful smile!

The annoying sound of the bell interrupted Jen's reminiscing. She kept her head down as the other students passed by her desk. She didn't want anyone to look at her; it was just better this way. When the room was almost empty, Jen yanked her bag from behind her chair, causing most of her stuff to fall on the floor. Sighing, she grabbed everything and bundled it in her arms, too upset to put it back in her bag. She hoped she could leave the classroom without Miss Pine noticing her.

Head down, walk fast! But Miss Pine was already heading to the door to cut her off.

Can't I just be left alone?

"Hold on a minute."

Dramatically rolling her eyes and sighing deeply, Jen looked up to face her cumbersome teacher.

Miss Pine kept her poise and calmly said, "Why do you daydream so often? This isn't like you. You don't belong here, you—"

"You're right about that! I don't belong here." Jen purposely cut her off just to make Miss Pine sound bad.

Miss Pine looked into Jen's sad blue eyes. "You know what I meant. You can pass this class, Jen. Things will get better. Just give it some time." With that, Miss Pine walked back to the mountain of papers that covered her desk.

Without saying another word, Jen hurried out of the classroom. She tried to make it to her locker, but the weight of the mocking eyes of the other students slowed her down. First, they simply smirked, and then came the comments.

"Hey, Jen," Lynette called as she flicked her long blond hair. She was the reason Jen had dropped cross-country.

Lynette was jealous that Jen was the better runner. When the disappearance of Jen's father became public, Lynette did what any selfish power hungry girl would do; she taunted Jen horribly and turned the other teammates against her by spreading vicious gossip about what really happened to John. Jen buckled from the pressure; Lynette stood proudly the day Jen was done in and threw her uniform in the school dumpster as she took off running for home.

"So, I heard you were daydreaming and had another outburst in class. Bad news travels fast," said Lynette, standing with her clique next to their lockers.

Jen didn't take another step. Every day since the news became known she'd received this sort of treatment and had suffered. She lowered her head, causing her hair to hang down so that her face was barely visible. She felt like simmering coals were being stirred from within her gut.

Feeling powerful, Lynette walked up to Jen until she was directly in front of her, and then mockingly asked, "Do you think you can hide behind your hair? You are such a pathetic freak!"

By this time, a ring of spectators had formed around them. Jen felt as if she were on fire.

Then, Lynette sneered. "With a weirdo like you for a daughter, it's no wonder your father left."

That did it. Looking at the books in her hands, Jen let her fury take control. Not stopping to think about the consequences or care for that matter, she hurled the books wildly at her tormentors as she screamed, "Shut up! Shut up, all of you!"

Papers and notebooks flew into the air. Lynette jumped to the side, but not before receiving a good whack across the side of the face from a hefty notebook. Her friends screamed and ducked to avoid the flying school books. Other onlookers that were out of harm's way stared and laughed at the outrageous scene before them. One book nearly hit Miss Pine in the head as she stormed out of her classroom to see what all the commotion was about.

"Miss Pine, Miss Pine!" cried Lynette. "Look! Jen's gone insane. Stop her!"

Miss Pine ran over and said, "That will be enough, Jennifer Hanning! Wait until the principal hears about this!"

Before the last paper hit the floor, Miss Pine walked off, pulling Jen by the arm to the office, leaving the scattered mess of her rage all over the hallway.

Chapter 2
Office Time

Miss Pine triumphantly marched Jen into the main office and walked straight up to the secretary's desk. The petite woman's brown bun jostled on the top of her head as she typed another monotonous daily report for the principal, completely ignoring the both of them until she was finished with her sentence on the computer. Only then did she look up at them with a raised eyebrow, staring at the both of them in utter annoyance.

"Can I help you with something?" she said nonchalantly.

"Yes, that would be nice. We need to see the principal right now," blurted Miss Pine.

The secretary sighed, pushed herself away from her desk and stood up. "Well, I'll see if he can see you, but he's a busy man so you may just have to wait for a while."

She walked over to his closed door and quietly let herself in. Within a minute, she was back out and approached them. "Well, it looks like he wants to see you right now." Irritation was evident in her voice.

Miss Pine didn't bother saying another word to her and waltzed Jen into the office.

The principal of Elmwood High remained seated behind his desk. His black leather chair faced the window that overlooked his prized courtyard. For a minute, he ignored both Miss Pine and Jen as they stood in his office. Then finally, Mr. Coogan rose from his chair, clasped his hands behind his back, and turned to address Jen.

"Jennifer Hanning, come look out this window with me."

With great diffidence, Jen slowly and squeamishly crept over to the window and gazed down at the school's giant diamond-shaped courtyard. At each point of the diamond was a gate that opened to a cobblestone path cutting straight through a beautifully landscaped garden. Silky pink tulips, velvety violets, ruby-red roses, and golden daffodils swayed rhythmically in the balmy breeze, creating a kaleidoscope of color. White lilies outlined the four paths that led to a gazebo in the center of the courtyard. The gazebo was carefully hand-crafted out of oak. Its sturdy base held a beautifully designed marble fountain. Water spouted from the top like a miniature geyser and then trickled gracefully down the almond-shaped bowls.

Jen longed to find her way to the gazebo and envisioned herself sitting serenely by the fountain. Mr. Coogan, however, had a strict rule that no student was allowed into that garden paradise, unless given special permission. And it was made clear that she would never be permitted.

After a moment of silence, the principal decided to share one of his great life lessons.

"Do you know what this garden represents, Jennifer?" Without waiting for her to answer, he continued, "It represents the reputation of my fine school. It's beautiful and orderly, and it takes the cooperation of everyone to keep it that way. One weed can ruin a whole garden. In the same way, one disruptive student can ruin the reputation of the whole school. I will not tolerate either one. Miss Pine, please give me the quick version of today's incident. Jennifer, you will sit in that chair, and I don't expect to hear a word out of you."

A numbness infused Jen's body as she walked back around the principal's desk, plopped herself down and slouched in the chair that he indicated. Strangely enough, Jen was actually relieved that Mr. Coogan hadn't asked to hear her side of the story. She had no desire to attempt to explain her actions and what had prompted them. The principal would never understand. So there Jen sat, listening to Miss Pine's account of notebooks flying across the hallway and textbooks crashing against the lockers, with special emphasis on the one that nearly hit her in the face. Jen winced when Miss Pine also mentioned Jen's daydreams and frequent outbursts in class.

"So you see, Mr. Coogan, the other students were frightened by Jennifer's outburst. On top of that, I simply can't get through to her in class. It's time she received stronger consequences for her behavior," Miss Pine finally concluded.

Mr. Coogan didn't respond right away, but instead glared at Jen and shook his head. Jen felt like a caged animal, stuck in a world spiraling out of control. She longed to escape to a place where she would again fit in.

After what seemed like an eternity, the principal announced his decision. "Well, a three-day in-school suspension should help put some sense back into you. Oh and let's not forget a month of janitor duties after the suspension," he added with a quaint smile on his face.

Picking up the phone on his desk, Mr. Coogan called his secretary back into his office.

"Miss Willow, did you contact Jennifer's mother?"

"Yes, sir, she said she'll be here in an hour to pick her up."

"Well, send Jennifer to the detention room until her mother arrives."

Within minutes, Jen was sitting in a wobbly wooden chair in front of a table, surrounded by four dull gray walls. On the wall directly in front of her hung several posters with sayings intended to inspire reluctant students to do their best. Jen read them, but the messages meant nothing to her. She had better things to worry about, like that dream. Why did she keep finding herself in the forest?

Well, at least now I won't be disturbed.

So, sitting all alone in the detention room, Jen let her mind drift off to that mysterious place in the forest.

Chapter 3
The Journey Home

Raindrops rolled down the windshield as tears trickled down Adriana's face. Jen and her mother stared blankly out the car window, not saying a word to each other, something that Jen had grown painfully used to.

Later, during their silent dinner, Jen recalled the way it used to be; laughing, talking, and enjoying one another's company. Now all that was heard was the constant drip of the leaky kitchen faucet. It was a daunting reminder that her father's to do list was left undone.

Running her fingers through her hair, Adriana sighed and said, "Just clear the table and go to your room. I'm going to bed." With that, she got up and walked to her bedroom. Jen waited until she heard it: the sound of that squeaky door reverberating throughout the entire house as it closed off her mother from the world and, more importantly, from Jen.

Jen wept while agonizing memories consumed her, and then wiped her face with a napkin as she thought about her parents and the fateful day that changed all of their lives.

Chapter 4
A Step Back In Time

Jen's parents, John and Adriana, met while in college. Outgoing and friendly, Adriana had short brown hair, deep blue eyes, and a smile that lit up her whole face. John first set eyes on her in the library. Adriana was sitting at one end of the table and John made it a point to always sit on the other end. He studied her intensity and beauty as she scribbled notes down in a binder. Unwilling to ignore this stranger anymore, she looked over at him and smiled. John was a tall, thin man with dark brown hair and dreamy eyes that couldn't help but to stare whimsically at her. His black horn-rimmed glasses gave him a scholarly look that Adriana secretly adored. After about an hour of smooth conversation, John got up his nerve to ask her out. And that was how it all started.

As they spent time together, Adriana discovered that John was a bit more reserved than she, but Adriana didn't care, for she'd fallen deeply in love with the man. His gentleness and charm swept her away. The couple soon married and after college, they moved to Elmwood because of a lab position that became available for John just outside of town.

Adriana found a law office position, but decided to work part-time because she'd become pregnant with Jen, their first and only child. So Jen was born and raised in the quaint town of Elmwood. The family lived happily together until that terrible evening…

....

The sun was half hidden behind the hills when Jen and her parents sat down to eat dinner. The aroma of pot roast, mashed potatoes, and peach pie filled the whole house. The three sat around the dinner table and shared their day together as a gentle breeze drifted in through the screen door. Adriana stared wistfully out the window and then turned to the huge mess in the kitchen.

Jen could tell that her mother needed to get out for a while. "Why don't you two go for a walk? I'll take care of the dishes tonight."

Adriana's eyes energetically lit up. She looked at her husband.

"Let's go, hon. We haven't been able to spend much time together with all the overtime you've had to put in at the lab."

John glanced at his lovely wife, who was staring at him pleadingly.

"That sounds great. Thanks, Jen," he replied.

"Don't mention it, Dad." Then she added, "Please don't go in the woods. You know people have been saying that something unnatural lives there."

John smiled and spoke gently to his overly concerned daughter. "Don't worry about us, Jen. When you get a little older, you'll realize you shouldn't believe everything you hear, especially superstitions. And you shouldn't let other people's opinions influence you, either."

Jen smiled. She'd always admired her father's self-assurance. John and Adriana rose from the table and walked toward the door. On their way out, John grabbed his small leather backpack and swung it around his shoulders. Adriana took his hand tenderly in hers and chuckled. "It's just a short walk, dear. You don't need to take that with you everywhere you go."

Inside the bag were a few items that were precious to John and had been passed down from generation to generation. His great-grandfather had fashioned the bag out of fine leather and put a gift in it for his son. But shortly after giving it to him, John's great-grandfather had disappeared and was never heard from or seen again.

Since the bag was the last thing he made before he went missing, it held great sentimental value. Eventually, John's father inherited it. He added a gift to the bag and gave it to his son on his eleventh birthday. Sadly, John's father passed away a year after that. Because of the sudden death of his father, John was especially attached to the pack and rarely left home without it.

"You know me, darling," was all he could say.

Adriana shook her head in surrender and the two left the house at half-past six.

"We'll be back in an hour, Jen," her father called as they walked down the porch steps.

"Okay, bye."

Knowing that her father was always prompt, Jen got to work on the kitchen right away, hoping to get it cleaned before her parents returned. She put her headphones in, clicked on her favorite playlist on her ipod, and quickly became lost in the music while she cleaned. It wasn't until she'd swept the kitchen floor and danced a bit to her music in the living room that Jen looked up to see the time: 8:30 p.m.

"What?"

She yanked off the headphones and dropped them with the ipod on the table as she ran out the door and looked down the street, hoping to see her parents strolling up the road, but there was no sign of them. There was no cause for alarm, but yet Jen was fighting the grip of a dreading panic.

You know you're overreacting. Calm yourself down!

The reassuring thoughts became useless with each passing minute. She ran inside and called a few of her parents' friends who lived nearby. She asked them if John and Adriana had stopped by for a quick visit, but in each case she was told they hadn't been there. Now Jen was really worried.

The last person Jen could think to ask was Old Sam who lived right next to the woods. His house was across the street and about a hundred yards down from theirs. Old Sam was the man who had started the stories of the voices in the woods. He said that he used to hear them call his name and say other strange things as well. Despite being ridiculously far-fetched, the stories spread like wildfire, and soon, many of the townspeople believed Old Sam's tales. People were warned to stay clear of the woods. Several teenagers who ventured in ran out screaming, claiming they'd heard strange voices calling their names. Old Sam became obsessed with the forest and said that it would one day destroy the world. When he crossed that bridge, everybody in the town grew a little fearful of him and decided it would be best if he were left alone.

With great trepidation, Jen tip-toed up the creaky wooden steps of Old Sam's ancient porch. The crooked screen door rested obliquely on its hinges. Jen took a deep breath and exhaled as she nervously knocked on the peeling wooden frame.

"Who there! I ain't buyin' nothin', so jus' lemme alone!"

"Mr. Sam, sir, it's me, your neighbor, Jennifer Hanning."

Jen looked hesitantly through a tear in the screen. She could see a solitary figure seated in the living room's only chair. The old wooden rocker creaked like a choir of pesky crickets.

Old Sam got up in a slow limp toward the door. His oversized, raggedy overalls were held up by a pair of tightly strapped suspenders in an attempt to make his clothes fit right. His aged, wrinkled face looked down at Jen.

"I'm just looking for my parents, sir. They went for a walk and no one has seen them. Have you seen them, Mr. Sam?" Jen asked politely.

What happened next gave Jen goose bumps. Old Sam threw back his head and laughed devilishly. When he stopped, he looked into her eyes and said, "Oh, I seen 'em awright, walk straight into thar doom I did. Thar gone, lil girl. Gone!"

In sheer fear and panic at his words, she walked backwards until she almost fell down the steps and then dashed home.

Jen burst through the screen door and called the police station for help, but they didn't seem to think that two grown-ups being gone for a couple of hours was a serious issue. Jen did her best to convince the sheriff otherwise.

"My parents said they'd be back in an hour, and they're never late. They went into the forest. I asked Old Sam, and he said he saw them go in, but he didn't see them cone out."

"Old Sam, heh? You're actually going to believe anything he says?"

"Old Sam might be crazy, but he would still know if he saw my parents go into the woods. Would you just please do your job and do something?" Jen said frantically.

The sheriff thought for a moment, and reluctantly said, "Well, I guess we'll come and check it out."

Slamming the phone down as hard as she could did little to appease her anger at the sheriff's apathy.

By 9:30 p.m., the sheriff arrived with a few of the townsmen and their hound dogs. The dogs went to work right away and sniffed for the trail of the missing couple. Picking up the scent, they ran until they reached the edge of the woods about a quarter of a mile from the Hannings' house. There they stood, barking at the forest's edge but refusing to go in. Several men traveled down the main paths of the forest, but there was no sign of the missing couple.

Jen sat on her porch steps while the search party stood in front of her house, discussing what to do next. Suddenly, Adriana appeared out of the black forest night. Her jeans and blue striped T-shirt were blood-stained and soaking wet and her silky brown hair was straggly and wild. She staggered a couple of steps toward the group, then fell to the ground and began to convulse.

Jen gasped when she saw the terrible condition her mother was in. She ran to her side, knelt down, and cradled her. "Mom! What happened to you? Where's Dad?"

Adriana sobbed and shook her head. Her lips quivered so much she could barely speak.

"He's…gone…into…the…light…he's…gone!" Adriana whimpered and then passed out.

The evening breeze diminished and fog rolled over the land. Sobbing, Jen sat in the grass, holding her mother. Since Adriana's face and arms were scratched and bleeding, the sheriff called for an ambulance.

Other members of the search party stood, shaking their heads. One man turned to another and whispered, "There's gotta be something in that forest we don't know about. I don't know about you but I ain't gonna be the first to volunteer in anymore searches." The other man looked at Adriana's condition and shook his head in agreement.

Two days later, Adriana regained consciousness. She lay in the hospital bed, oblivious to the world around her. Those that were brave formed search parties and repeatedly went out to look for John, but he was nowhere to be found and Adriana was released from the hospital and returned home to be with her daughter.

A couple of weeks after the incident, while Adriana and Jen were resting on the swing in front of their house, Adriana finally spoke to Jen about that terrible night.

"I can't tell you what happened, Jen. I don't really understand it myself. It was just the woods, and then came the light. Why did he have to follow? It was…it was….," Adriana's voice trailed off. Then a look of sheer terror crossed her face and she lashed out bitterly, "I never want to talk about it! And never go near those woods, Jen, not ever!"

Tears streamed down Jen's face instantly. Just when she thought she would get answers from the only person that knew anything, her mother selfishly bottled up.

"Mom, please," Jen sobbed, "you're the only one who knows anything and I know that whatever it was, it was bad. But please, I miss him and I've been patient. Won't you tell me?"

The pleading went unheard. Adriana had become stiff and indignant to her daughter and her pain. "Promise me, Jen," she coldly insisted.

"Fine, I promise."

"Good…good." Adriana got up from the swing and went inside the house.

I just have to give her more time. She'll tell me. I'm her daughter. She'll tell me in time.

Jen didn't push her mom anymore about it in hopes that her mother would open up soon for her daughter's sake. But Adriana never spoke concerning her father's bizarre disappearance.

In time, the townspeople ventured into the woods, hoping to find answers themselves, or perhaps even to find John's body if it was out there.

All searches came up empty and with questions left unanswered; they turned to Adriana and demanded the story, but she refused to talk. She took a job outside of town to avoid all of them. Her continued silence turned friends into enemies as the gossip reigned for a season throughout the town. The lack of work and one income was quickly bringing the family to the brink of bankruptcy. And Jen gave up hope altogether. She had lost her father to a mystery, her mother to insanity, and her friends to gossip. There was nothing left to hope for.

....

So, there Jen sat, alone at the table across from her mother's empty chair. She dried her tears, cleared the table and turned off the lights. She dragged herself to her room, and not bothering to change out of her jeans and gray-hooded pullover, she plopped on the bed. Deep down inside, she hoped that her mother's door would open and she would come and sit down next to her, hug her and love her, but a cold and painful bitterness swept across her heart as she knew that would never happen. After several minutes, Jen fell fast asleep.

Chapter 5
Once Fictitious, Now Undeniable

Once again, Jen found herself standing at the edge of the forest, staring down the crooked path, barely visible and mostly overgrown. The wind pushed against her back and softly whispered her name. She could no longer fight it. Lifting her arms in surrender, she let the wind pick her up. It carried her over the path of the forest and finally set her down in a small clearing. In the dead center stood the most bizarre tree Jen had ever laid eyes on. Its twisted trunk curved like a wild river and its branches were full of leaves of different sizes and shapes. A peace emanated from it.

"It's time, Jen. It's time!"

....

A click and a squeak caused Jen's eyes to pop open. It was the sound of her mother's door opening. Jen closed her eyes and pretended to be asleep. Adriana peeked in her daughter's room for a few moments and then tiptoed across the living room, through the kitchen, and out the back door. As soon as Jen heard her mother leave, she jumped out of bed, put on her shoes, grabbed her flashlight from her desk drawer, and headed toward the back door. Looking out a window, Jen felt a flash of anger and fear when she saw her mother run down the road and venture into the forest.

Really! How could she keep this from me?

With a newfound determination spawned on by anger, Jen was

determined to find out from her mother by the end of the night what was really going on. Jen stepped outside. Her pulse quickened as she stared at the forest that had ripped her family apart.

"This ends tonight," she spoke under her breath, ran down the porch steps and hurried after her mother.

Before she knew it, Jen reached the forest's edge. The towering trees blocked out most of the moonlight. With the wind urgently pushing against her back, Jen started down the dark and gloomy path that lay before her.

Little beady eyes stared intently through the bushes as this stranger plodded along the trail that wound its way intricately through the thick brush. The animals that made their home in this forest were unaccustomed to seeing humans creep through their territory, until recently. They kept their distance from this unwelcome newcomer.

Jen used her flashlight and inched forward, looking for any small branches hanging over the ground so she wouldn't trip. She came to a point where the trail split into three different directions. When Jen peered down the path farthest to the right, a chilling gust of wind blew from that direction and brushed against her face. The flashlight went out, and Jen dropped it on the ground.

"Just great! Now how am I gonna find her?" Jen protested out loud.

Trying not to panic, Jen breathed slowly for a minute, and then groped her way for a few yards down the trail that led to the left, until she tripped over a large root. Scrambling to get up, she noticed a faint light zipping around further down the trail.

That's got to be Mom! Jen rushed toward the light, hoping to catch up to her mother. Jen kept herself from calling out to her, even though she wanted to so badly, but then there was that other side of her that wanted to sneak up on her and catch her in the act of her secrecy.

She walked fast, and then switched to a jog. Before she knew it, she was running. Her eyes fixed on nothing but the light. Without her realizing it, the light empowered her and Jen was running at a dead sprint. When it veered off the path, Jen went with it. She was running fast, jumping logs, ducking under branches, dodging rocks and trees as if it were the middle of the day. The hypnotic light led Jen deeper and deeper into the forest.

She ran until she came to a clearing, and then froze, for the light had come to a stop. Then it vanished completely. Jen's senses returned, and she became painfully aware of how long and hard she'd been running. Her clothes were drenched with sweat and she needed a minute to catch her breath.

After the breathing was under control, Jen wiped the beads of sweat from her brow with the back of her hand, and trudged into the clearing, but stopped abruptly. There, looming in front of her was the uncanny tree with its twisted trunk and leaves of all shapes and sizes. The last dream stopped here, so Jen waited in great anticipation.

It didn't take long before her eyes drifted down to the tree's base, and she gasped at what she saw there: her father's small leather backpack! She ran to it and, falling to her knees, grabbed the sack and held it tightly against her chest. The wind picked up again, pushing the clouds out of the way to reveal the full moon, which gave more light. The rustling leaves seemed to whisper her name. Jen jumped to her feet and backed away from the tree, hoping her ears were playing tricks on her. The wind whistled again and, this time, the sound of her name was much more distinct.

"Jennifer." The voice came from within the light that glowed from the trunk of the tree. It sounded like that of a woman calling out in gentle reassurance.

Jen stood paralyzed in fear, and trembled. All she could do was clutch her father's backpack tightly to her chest. Once more the wind blew, but now it came more forcefully as if a storm were fast approaching. The moonlight shone directly upon the tree. Immediately, the bark split apart. Light exploded from within the hollow section.

"Jennifer, do not be afraid."

Jen shielded her eyes and stood there, anchored in fear.

This can't be real! Jen, please wake up, anytime now!

With knees knocking, she held her breath until she felt faint. Then just like in her dream, a wave of peace flowed out of the circular brilliance of light. It filled Jen, making her one with its tranquility. The wave slowly receded, taking her fears away. With a new sense of inner peace, Jen spoke to the mysterious anomaly. "How do you know my name?"

"Your father, John," the being within the tree responded.

"My father!" A storm of furious emotions surged through her and she lashed out, "So it was you! You're the one that took my father away! I don't care what you are; I should burn you down to the ground!"

The being's respondent light instantaneously turned deep yellow, and then softly spoke, "I'm sorry for all the pain you have suffered, Jen. It wasn't my intention or my desire to hurt you. I was here in this spot, talking with your father before your mother came. We needed his help and the help of his family, for we are at war and Earth is in more danger than it knows. When your mother came, she was irate and refused to listen to her husband. She grabbed his arm and tried yanking him away, but she fell backwards and John fell into the light and was transferred to our world. It happened so suddenly, the power of the portal faded and I could no longer stay and disappeared from her, leaving her screaming."

Jen swung her head from side to side at the thought of her father fighting in some war. She only wanted one thing—for her father to come home. Tears stained her face as she pleaded desperately with the tree. "Please, bring him back to me. We have military and others trained for war. We are no help to you. Can you please just send him back now?"

"Daughter of John, how I wish I could." The glow in the tree began to sway like the waves of an ocean on a calm summer day. Jen was hit again with the peace that she'd felt moments before. She once again surrendered her anger to the waves within this mysterious light.

"I have beckoned you here because your father is missing in action. We lost contact with him during his last mission. We need your help to find him."

Jen laughed out loud uncontrollably, "Excuse me? You expect me to find him? If you can't find him, then how am I supposed to? I wouldn't even know where to begin, and you look a whole lot more powerful than me!"

"I can show you where to begin if you come with me into my dimension of Tranquil Earth. I am unable to find him, for it requires his own flesh and blood to help."

"Tranquil Earth? You mean Earth, right? Like another country in Earth, or maybe the Bermuda Triangle?"

"No, Jen, I am talking about another Earth. There's one Earth that exists, but there are multiple dimensions of it. Within this intra-dimensional reality is my world, Tranquil Earth. My name is Hope, and I am the gateway between our worlds. Unfortunately, the passageway through me is collapsing. If you desire to find your father, you must come with me now."

Still standing in shock, Jen held her father's bag in front of her, and then asked solemnly, "So, is my dad really lost in some other dimension?"

"Yes."

Though Jen was still processing the news in shock, knowing that her father could be in danger was better than knowing nothing, and that somewhat gave her hope again and settled her decision.

"I'll find him. Just tell me what to do, but promise me that you will come back for my mother and be fast about it. When she finds I am gone, she'll have a heart attack."

"I will do everything in my power to come back to this spot and not give up until we have her safe with us. Now quickly, walk toward the light in the tree. Within seconds, it will shift you into my dimension. Before you go, let me tell you that when you reach the other side, I will not be there. Because the power of evil is so strong, I'm limited as to the exact place where you will appear when you enter my world. I'm sending Iyon, a Warrior Horse, to find and protect you. You can trust him. He will take you where you need to go."

The light changed from deep yellow back to brilliant white and began to flicker violently.

"The passageway between our worlds is closing. You must come now!"

With no more time to talk, Jen strapped on her father's small backpack, walked toward the tree, and then disappeared into the light.

Chapter 6
The Journey Begins

The warm glow enveloped Jen and drew her into the portal. A tight pressure squeezed her body, and a wave of heat traveled through her. The transfer was brief—the length of a normal deep breath. She was thrown into Tranquil Earth, landing on a plot of cushiony grass in the center of a gigantic field. She rolled onto her stomach and pushed herself up onto her knees.

Jen looked down and studied the blades of grass. She paused for a moment when she realized how different this world was. Instead of the blades being green and filled with life, this grass was black as death itself. The sight horrified her, and she jumped up to face the tree.

"What's this...?" Jen abruptly stopped speaking, realizing it was just a plain tree. She'd forgotten for a second that the voice had said she wouldn't be there. She was all alone in this strange world.

Jen's gaze shifted from the tree's trunk to its leaves, and she noticed that they were black like the grass. She grabbed one of the leaves, yanked it off, and rubbed it between her thumb and finger. It felt no different than her green leaves back home. Looking up, she saw the sky was blanketed with violet clouds, giving a strange tint to the land. The field was surrounded by trees. There was no way of telling which way she should go.

Suddenly, a faint flicker of light caught Jen's attention from out of the corner of her eye. She turned to her right and waited to see if it would appear again. There it was! The light was twinkling way off in the distance, but then vanished. *Could that be Iyon?* Waiting around wouldn't help her father, so she hastened toward the light she had seen. Massive hills loomed in the distance. Anxious to find this Warrior Horse, Jen quickened her pace.

Chapter 7
The Skeign, the Hunt, and the Daring Jump

In the center of this unfathomable world lay Tran, the capital city. On its south side was a deep valley. To the north was a forest that extended for many miles and gradually expanded to the east and west. Before the invasion, Tran was a beautiful and peaceful city, but now it was fortified with towering metallic walls that had no entry gates. In the center, an ancient enemy dwelt who went by the name of Dolorous. He was a formless black entity that could take the shape of a dragon if it so desired, and dwelled inside a giant circular temple. The temple had eight strong pillars engraved with repulsive gargoyles. A long stone staircase led to the top of the temple. Dolorous, who now controlled this world, had the power to decide who could leave and who must stay in this prison-like city.

The captured citizens of this once great city were controlled and bound to serve Dolorous, whose main source of energy and strength came from their hopelessness. They were forced to live in over-populated warehouses filled with cages. Free will was abolished as these inhabitants had become nothing more than mindless beings that would slowly wither away into nothing as Dolorous sucked their life and energy. This ancient dragon took great pleasure from seeing them suffer, and their hopelessness gave power ultimately to the Master.

Standing upon the stone steps of the temple were the vicious creatures collectively called the Skeign. Their bodies, covered with thick oily black fur, were the size of horses, yet their forms resembled lions. Long razor-sharp claws protruded from their paws. Tentacles, with iron hooked tips that could shoot bolts of electrical power and poison into their prey, projected from their tails. Their faces were covered with sensors that allowed them to detect individuals still with hope and life. With their bat-like wings, they traveled to and fro throughout their world, obeying Dolorous' every command.

Shortly after the tree spewed Jen into the dimension of Tranquil Earth, the Skeign's sensors went off. They opened their saber-toothed mouths and let out a hideous roar that echoed throughout the entire city. In unison, they turned toward Dolorous, bowed down, and waited for their orders.

After Dolorous manifested itself as a thunder cloud, it began to transform into a black hole. Then it spoke to the Skeign in a guttural voice. "That cursed being has found another one from True Earth. Go! Find this human and bring her to me! For she is the one we have been foretold about and must be destroyed. We will let no human thwart the Master's great plan! Now go find her and bring her to me!"

With that, the Skeign collectively bowed their heads and flew off, screeching and howling. Once they departed, Dolorous shrunk itself down to its original form and spoke to the wind, "You won't be successful in your mission. I will find you and suck that hope right from your soul. I…will…find…you…. I…will…destroy..you!" Dolorous laughed deviously while its clouds thundered from within.

....

As Jen approached the forest's edge, the wind suddenly changed. A chilling gust swept through, and with it came a thunderous voice that bellowed, "I…will…find…you…!" The wind surrounded Jen, and she was overcome by fear and hopelessness. Then negative thoughts infiltrated and filled her mind.

You know you're nothing but a helpless girl and a fool. Who do you think you are, coming into my realm? I will find you, Jen, and it will be our pleasure to slowly devour your pathetic soul!

Jen sank to her knees and gasped for breath. Out of desperation she rasped, "Iyon, find me!" She fell to the ground, paralyzed. Vibrations. Vibrations of something powerful headed her way. *Please be Iyon!* Jen thought as she slipped into unconsciousness.

....

Iyon, a Warrior Horse, was a creature filled with ancient power, possessing abilities way beyond human comprehension. He had the capability of producing bursts of heat and energy that could destroy a multitude of foes at once. His razor-sharp hooves could cut through any substance if need be. His powerful tail, when snapped, sounded like a thousand whips and emitted bolts of electricity and blue radiant power from each individual strand. And then there were his blue eyes full of unfathomable mystery and unexplainable abilities. Being able to sense humans and other creatures from hundreds of miles away, Iyon would search out and rescue those who were not yet imprisoned by evil.

Not too long ago, Iyon had been one of many Warrior Horses. They had been the protectors of their world and had taken great pride in guarding Hope, the Life Source of Tranquil Earth, until the arrival of Dolorous, the Death Force. Hope was a beautiful glowing beam that radiated all the colors of the rainbow or could change to any one color completely, depending on emotion. For centuries, she had stationed herself at the center of Tran.

The Warrior Horses had also been the Gate Keepers of this once glorious city, admitting only the pure of heart. Tran's walls were originally made of marble, with gates of gold decorated with intricate designs of ivory. This paradise once had cobblestone streets lined with exotic trees of unknown origin where beautiful birds of all kinds and colors nested. Along the sides of the road were gardens full of many flowers and bushes that blossomed year round. All streets led to the center of town bustling with life. The people there had thrived peacefully and had worked together in harmony to make their city flourish. When the sun set, energy would flow out of Hope and fill all the lamps in the city with a soft white glow, making the night almost as bright as the day if need be.

And then came that dreadful day. As the Warrior Horses stood at their posts, monitoring the gates, a massive storm cloud came out of nowhere and formed in the valley that lay before the city. The black clouds twisted and turned violently, sending out flashes of black lightning. The Warrior Horses sounded the alarm. They rushed out of the city, sealing the gates behind them. Sensing the approach of pure evil, they stood ready to protect Tran from this assault. An army of hideous Skeign flew out of the black cloud. Their bodies and bat-like wings darkened the land. The clouds thundered so loudly that the sound reverberated for hundreds of miles. The ominous spinning mass generated the power of many tornadoes and then transformed itself into a black hole. Acting as a vortex, this black hole drew all hope and free-will into its abyss. Before they knew what was happening, the sentinels of Tran were overcome by misery and sorrow. The Warrior Horses, though greatly weakened, fought valiantly, but the powerful oppression and the great multitude of the Skeign overcame them. Many were slain and other Warrior Horses were captured and ferreted away to become eternal prisoners.

Iyon watched in horror as his fellow Guardians were slain. Knowing what now must be done, Iyon bolted through a secret door in the wall and raced to Hope's side. As he sprinted through the city, he noticed people lying all over the streets. Although Tran had not yet been breached by the Skeign or Dolorous, their evil was so potent that it was already overpowering the citizens. Desperately wanting to protect Hope, Iyon galloped all the faster until he reached her.

Immediately upon his arrival, Hope said, "Quickly, Iyon, we've no time to lose! Follow me."

Iyon nodded sadly and followed the wondrous circle of light through an underground tunnel that led to the northern woods far beyond the city, where the ancient trees proudly blanketed the gentle slopes. A band of city people, mostly women and children and a band of soldiers to protect them, escaped, staying close to Hope for protection from the oppression. There, under one of the oldest trees in the forest, Iyon stood facing Hope. Her color changed from brilliant white to deep yellow. Then Iyon saw a golden collar float out of Hope, along with a gem containing all the colors that she emitted. This gem was also filled with a secret and ancient power that none could see or comprehend. The golden collar was placed on Iyon, and the gem was magically split in two. One half became imbedded in the collar, and the other quickly returned to Hope's glow.

"This collar and gem will shield you from the forces of evil and will give you a higher power when you need it. The ruthless dragon, Dolorous, and his army of Skeign have infiltrated our world and now, our city. You need to rescue as many of our citizens as possible, Iyon. Find them and bring them to Tolare, the secret place where they'll remain undetected and safe. The gem in the golden collar will guide you there. I'll enter the dimension of True Earth and see if I can find the ones able to save our world. We both know what's at stake here."

Hope's glow reverted back to white. The tree's trunk pulled apart, and she entered, and then added, "I had hoped this day would not come, but the dawn of darkness is upon us. I must go into hiding in Tolare, but I will help you in every way I can. Please be careful, for I can sense that you're the last Warrior Horse. Now go! Go quickly my friend, and be safe!" With that, Hope imprisoned herself within the tree and at that time, was able to transport the refugees that were there with her safely to Tolare. When that was done, the trunk of the ancient tree closed and returned to its original form.

Shortly thereafter, Dolorous completed his takeover of Tran. The marble walls changed to granite, and their golden gates disappeared. The inhabitants transformed into mindless automatons. The green in all the grass, leaves, and stems turned to venomous ebony, and gloomy violet clouds rolled in as the power of evil transformed their world.

Iyon bravely journeyed throughout Tranquil Earth, seeking survivors and carrying them to safety. He frequently encountered the Skeign and battled over remaining souls. His numerous victories and his ability to evade capture enraged Dolorous and his legion. He had become a pestilent thorn to the ancient dragon. He could not defeat or capture Iyon and lost many in his army when he tried.

Iyon fearlessly continued his crusade until the day he received the message from Hope as he was roaming through the forest. "I have found the daughter of John! Hurry, Iyon, and find her!" Already sensing her presence, Iyon took off in search of Jen.

....

Iyon knew that time to find Jen was short and he could not allow the enemy to capture her, at any cost. Charging through the forest, he searched desperately. As the feeling of her presence strengthened, he ran at an incredible speed. He could also sense the enemy approaching her as well. His ears pricked back and he increased his stamina, preparing himself for imminent battle.

Jumping through the last of the brush, Iyon landed at the edge of a field. Looking around, he spotted a girl lying unconscious on the ground and galloped over to her. The gem on Iyon's collar lit up. He took one steady breath in and exhaled gently over her, creating a ring of blue energy that destroyed the witchcraft that enslaved her. The oppression lifted. Opening her eyes, Jen looked straight up, and beheld a magnificent white stallion resembling a horse but so much more. His appearance fascinated her deepest imagination. His radiant white mane, blown by the wind, looked like tongues of white fire framing his head. But his piercing navy blue eyes, glowing with intensity, stood out the most. Never before had she seen eyes like that on a horse. Peering into them, she could sense great power from within him.

"Iyon?" But immediately, she felt silly for asking a horse a question.

"Yes, Jen, I am Iyon whom the being in the tree told you about."

Taken aback in shock, she exclaimed, "You can talk?"

"Yes. There are many things about this world that are different from your world. I don't have time to explain right now. We must go to a safer place to talk before the Skeign arrive. We must leave this place immed…" Iyon's words were swallowed up by the horrific screeching of the Skeign. The horde rampaged through the forest and appeared on the opposite side of the field. Iyon's eyes flashed all shades of blue when he saw the flaming red eyes of his hated enemy staring hungrily back at him off in the distance.

Iyon knelt down. "Get on! Hurry!"

Sitting up, Jen peeked around Iyon and saw beasts racing at a frightening pace toward them. Spurred on by fear, she jumped to her feet, flung her leg over Iyon's back, and grabbed the collar as tightly as she could. Iyon darted into the blackness of the forest. Howling and growling, the Skeign bolted across the field and into the forest in pursuit. Their hatchet-like claws chopped through branches and even small trees as they chased their prey. A band of Skeign took to the sky while others pursued Iyon and Jen on the ground.

Petrified, Jen clutched the collar with all her might which in return gave her the strength she needed to stay on Iyon's back as they charged through the forest. She glanced behind her to see the creatures hot on their trail. Her eyes filled with disgust and horror as she got a glimpse of the hideousness of the enemy.

"Iyon! They're right behind us!"

The chase took them deeper into the forest where the leaves on the trees created a black canopy. Whenever there was a break in the canopy, the airborne Skeign swooped down like hawks going in for the kill. Iyon thrashed his metallic tail madly, whipping bolts of electricity at the enemy as they attempted to snatch Jen off his back. Knowing they could not return empty handed, the legion multiplied into the hundreds, coming now from almost all directions.

"They're right on top of us! No, they're everywhere! What are we going to do?"

"Don't worry. We're almost to the Death Drop. I'm going to jump, Jen. It is easy to out-fly these creatures."

"What! A Death Drop?"

"Just hang on!"

Jen screamed continuously as Iyon, eyes blazing of blue fire, shot out rays of heat and energy, eradicating any of the Skeign that got too close to Jen. At full stride, Iyon broke through the forest's edge and leaped off the cliff. A pack of Skeign were waiting there in the air and tried to pounce on Iyon and rip Jen from his back, but Iyon anticipated their sloppy strategy and eradicated the entire flock in the air within a matter of a second.

The gem around his neck beamed as they flew down into the canyon that extended for hundreds of miles known as Dodger's Edge. Iyon twisted and turned skillfully through the sharp and deadly curves while the Skeign flew clumsily behind, many of them dashing themselves against the jagged cliffs, unable to twist and turn as Iyon could. If it hadn't been for the power of the gem holding Jen in place, she would have been thrown off and dashed against the rocky walls. The chase in the air didn't last long, for Iyon was too skillful and fast for the Skeign. He lost them through the maze of rocks deep in the canyon. After a hopeless search, the Skeign landed on the ledges of many cliffs, covering them like a thick blanket of black pesky bats, and roared in both anger and fear, shaking their heads from side to side in yet another shameful defeat. Dolorous would not be pleased with their returning empty-handed. The fiends had no choice but to go back and face the wrath of their master. With heads hung low, they flew away in silence.

Chapter 8
Tolare

For miles and miles, Iyon wended his way through the sharp curves of the canyon. With ease and perfection, he maneuvered every one. Suddenly, Jen saw a sheer cliff rising into the clouds. She screamed and closed her eyes as Iyon flew straight into the rocky wall. Then her body jerked forward as she felt Iyon come to a complete stop. There was no impact, no noise, nothing at all.

Jen opened her eyes and saw a magnificent sight. Iyon was standing on a crystal platform suspended in midair. They stood inside an enormous cavern with beautiful multicolored gems embedded in its walls. The crystal platform began to lower. While Jen hung on to Iyon's mane, she watched in child-like fascination as the brightly colored gems were illuminated by a strong green light that came from far below them. The light from below bounced off the embedded gems, making the appearance of dancing rainbows from one side of the cavern to the other. Jen looked down to see what the mysterious green light was, but the crystal platform was translucent and she could not see through it. Like an excited child, her heart pounded with anticipation as the power of the green glow intensified, causing the rainbows to dance all the more in front of her.

Finally, the platform lowered and the source of the glow was revealed. A giant emerald, many times the size of Iyon, hovered in the air. The platform stopped when it reached the same level as the emerald. Jen was mesmerized as her eyes remained transfixed on this rare jewel. An image gradually formed at its center as if she were watching a movie playing before her. It showed Earth. Next, stars appeared, blanketing the space around Earth. The sun shone way off in the distance. It was a beautiful picture of her galaxy, her home, but then a band of blackness overcame the planets. The darkness expanded, enveloping the sun and the stars. It advanced toward the Earth. Slowly, the evil wrapped around the entire planet until it could no longer be seen.

The purpose of the phenomenon eluded Jen, leaving her perplexed. Iyon said nothing concerning what had just transpired.

Did he even see it, or was it for my eyes only? Before Jen could say anything, the platform resumed its quick descent, and she and Iyon continued their journey in silence.

After a little while longer, they reached the bottom of the cavern. Iyon pranced off the platform and headed straight for a golden archway. It glowed so brightly that Jen had to shield her eyes. As the light faded, the doors opened slowly, and the two approached the hidden city that lay deep under the cliffs of Dodger's Edge.

This city was like a miniature version of Tran as it had been back in its glory days, minus the city walls, of course. As they emerged from the tunnel, Jen noticed off to the right of the pathway was a small forest full of fruit bearing trees. To the left were fields with cabins that looked like little islands amongst a sea of grain and many vegetable and fruit gardens. The laughter of children and the chirping of birds filled the air. Jen gazed all around in amazement.

"Where are we?"

"This is Tolare, the city of refuge. All of the refugees have come here to escape Dolorous and the Skeign."

"The Skeign being the black, ugly, lion-looking creatures?"

"That is them."

The sun shone brightly in the blue sky far above them. Jen tilted her head back, allowing the warm rays to caress her face.

"Iyon, how is all of this possible? What's with the sun and the sky when

I know we are underground?"

"We are inside the mountains. Look up again and I'll show you the light source of Tolare."

When the gem in Iyon's collar began to glow, the sky above them disappeared. In place of it appeared thousands of prisms rotating in mid-air. As the glow of the gem faded, the sky returned to its original state. Jen was awestruck by the continual wonders of this world.

Iyon sensed how she felt and broke the silence. "The people here enjoy the beauty and safety of Tolare. They live with the hope that one day the evil in this world will be defeated and all of Tranquil Earth will go back to normal. You, too, must hang on to hope, Jen, the hope that you will find your father." He then trotted down the path that led to the heart of the village.

As she turned to follow him, Jen took this moment to ponder all that had happened to her over the past several months. Memories of life without her father, as well as the deterioration of her relationship with her mother because of it, flashed through her mind. She was haunted by images of the townspeople of Elmwood staring at her as they whispered and laughed behind her back. In addition to all that, she'd witnessed a talking tree, a flying horse, and a world full of both horrible and majestic creatures. Jen wondered what could possibly happen next or what wonders still lay in store. Then she was plagued by a question that came from the depths of her heart.

"Why me?" Jen mouthed silently to herself.

"All will be explained shortly, Jen," Iyon said as they entered the village.

Jen cocked her head in surprise. "You heard me?"

"Mhmm."

As Iyon and Jen passed through the village, the people stopped working, looked at the two of them and nodded respectfully. Jen noticed that the expressions on many of their faces reflected relief.

One little girl wearing an exquisite peach garment ran and grabbed Jen's leg. Jen looked down at the little girl, who was no more than six, and their eyes met. Her darling face appeared so young, yet her eyes showed knowledge of pain and loss. As she continued to hold onto Jen, the expression in the child's eyes changed.

"I know you've come to help us. Don't be afraid," said the child. The little girl's mother called to her. "Jasmine, come back here."

The young one released Jen and skipped back to her mother. As Iyon continued toward the temple, Jasmine couldn't help herself, and called out one more time, "Don't be afraid!"

Chapter 9
House of Dahlia

As Iyon and Jen entered the temple in the center of the city, they were greeted by a band of soldiers dressed for battle. The soldiers stood at attention in several lines of ten, facing their commander. Their attire fascinated Jen, for their armor, including the protectors around their arms and legs, was made of a metallic material that Jen could not recognize. Sheathed weapons hung at their sides. However, Jen couldn't tell whether they were guns, swords or something else.

The commander saluted and called out, "Iyon!"

"Jared," Iyon replied.

The light brown-haired handsome young man smiled and said, "It's good to have you back. I see your mission was successful." Turning to Jen, he respectfully said, "My name is Jared, and it's an honor to meet you, Miss Jennifer."

Shocked by his greeting, Jen wasn't sure how to respond. So she simply nodded her head and said, "Thank you."

Jared turned back to Iyon. "We have good news. While you were away, we found another survivor and brought him here. He has valuable information that might prove very helpful to us."

Iyon nodded his head in approval. "Well done, Jared. I look forward to talking with him later."

With Jen still on his back, Iyon stepped a few paces away from Jared until he was standing in the middle of a circular pattern on the floor. The soldiers stayed in their formation and moved back until everyone had moved out of the circular pattern embedded in the floor. Iyon's front left hoof pressed down at the dead center of the circle. Immediately, the entire circle began spinning clockwise as it descended below ground level. Jen looked up and saw that another circular patterned stone had moved in the old one's place, sealing them off from the light and the rest of the world. For a moment, they were in utter darkness. She felt as if she and Iyon were floating in an abyss, making it impossible for her to tell if they were moving or standing still, which nauseated her stomach.

A faint yellow glow appeared. It increased in intensity until it lit up the entire room. Jen squinted and rubbed her eyes until they adjusted. Then she saw the source of the light. It was Hope and her glow was filling the center of a leafless tree suspended in midair. Even the roots swayed freely beneath the tree.

From within the illumination came Hope's soothing and reassuring voice. "I'm glad you're here, Jen. I am the true Life Source of Tranquil Earth." As Jen listened, she filled with more strength and confidence than she'd experienced for quite some time.

For the next few minutes, Hope explained what their world had been like before Dolorous and the vicious Skeign attacked it. She spoke of how Tran had been invaded, how its beauty had been destroyed, and how the souls of all the inhabitants had been enslaved. Dolorous' reign soon spread throughout their entire world, and Tolare became the only place where people were free from the bondage of darkness.

"One night, as I was desperately searching for someone to help us, I found a man and I knew he was special. He followed the glowing light as you did, and when he saw me, he showed no fear, only wonder and curiosity. Adriana caught up to your father and saw me as well. While your father was with us he never stopped worrying about the both of you and I promised him that I would continue searching for a way back to your town and somehow reunite your family. Know that I am sorry for the pain and grief you and your mother have had to endure. But Jen, while your father was with us, he helped us greatly in many ways."

Tears rolled down Jen's cheeks. She took a moment to collect herself and said, "I don't understand. Why couldn't you have come back in another tree near our house sooner than you did?"

"Although I can transport myself to your world, I have little control over where I'll end up when I get there. I tried many times to re-enter, but I failed to return to that same spot until recently. I was able to call to you in your dreams in hopes that we would be drawn to one another, and find each other we did. I tried the same with your mother, but sometimes, grown adults can be much more difficult to reach as they become set in their ways. But I will continue to work on this without cease."

"What about all the townspeople's rumors of hearing strange voices in the forest; weren't those voices your doing?"

"I know nothing about that, for I was near your town only two times. That is alarming news, and I don't know what it means, but I'll look into it. Let's concentrate on your father for now. His last location was in the dimension of Shadow Earth, a place that has long since been conquered by Felonious, one of the higher ranking officers of our sworn enemy."

Wanting to get to the bottom of things faster, Jen spoke quickly and interrupted her explanation, "Okay, wait a minute. Perhaps it's just my age, but I still don't understand; you keep mentioning different Earths. What do you mean? I'm from Earth, so where exactly am I?"

"My dear, you are on Earth."

Feeling a little vexed, Jen gazed into the light. "That's impossible. I know my own planet, and this is not Earth."

"The world you live in is indeed Earth, but we call it True Earth, for it's the central point that links all of our dimensions. What happens in one world affects the balance of good and evil in all the worlds of Earth. The world you're in right now is Tranquil Earth. For hundreds of years, the balance of power was in our favor, but this is no longer true. Something has happened, and now the forces of evil have a strong foothold in our worlds and are seeking to conquer them. If they succeed in defeating us and the last of the free worlds, then they will surely triumph over True Earth as well.

"Your father joined our ranks in the fight to save all the worlds of Earth. Recently, he felt compelled to go to the darkest of all places to find out what was drawing him. I told him of the dangers, but nothing I said would change his mind. I felt that if something was tugging at him that strongly, then it had to have come from a source higher than the man himself, so I let him go.

"He gathered a group of soldiers and went on a reconnaissance mission to Shadow Earth. Upon his return, he drew us maps of where he had been and wrote accounts of what he had seen. After the success of that mission, he and his troops went on several others. Tragically, neither your father nor any of his brave men came back from their last mission. Our only hope of finding John lies in you. You are his daughter and, once in Shadow Earth, you two should be drawn to one another.

"You see, your father had an amazing way of traveling while in Shadow Earth. It was through his mind's eye, if you will. He realized through much practice that when he envisioned a place, he would appear there. No one else has ever had that unique ability. It's our great hope that you too will have that gift. And if so, you should be able to find your father and his men."

"So, in order to find out if I have that ability, you have to send me there so I can try for myself?"

"Yes, that's the only way. Are you ready to accept a mission like this?"

Jen paused for a moment. *It's official; my version of reality is officially gone.* "Okay, let's give it a shot."

"I promise I will do everything in my power to find your mother and bring her safely to Tolare, but first things first, you need rest from your journey and new clothes as well. Iyon will take you to a cabin for the remainder of the day and we will meet back here early in the morning."

"I'm fine to go, really; why waste any more time if he's in some kind of danger?" Jen retaliated.

"So much like your father, you are. John is more resourceful than you know. And a weary traveler for such a mission would put both of you at risk. The wise thing will be to go early in the morning."

Jen realized this was a pointless argument so she bit her lip. *Guess she's not gonna listen to the voice of reason.*

The stone lifted at the same time that the one above them moved to the side, letting Iyon and Jen back above ground.

"So," Jen said reluctantly, "where are we headed to?"

With a playful snort in return, Iyon reared up and said, "To the house of Dahlia, of course! Now hold on."

"I don't like what that means!" Jen ended with another scream as Iyon took one massive leap into the air and within seconds, they were soaring over the village to the cabin just over the hill, right outside the hustle and bustle of the people and their 'city-life'.

Iyon made sure to gracefully land on the path just short of Dahlia's home and walked the rest of the way in.

"Any chance you can warn me next time you do that?" Irritation was evident in her voice.

"No."

"No? Really?"

"Really."

"You know, for a Warrior Horse, you sure got a lot of spunk and attitude," Jen proclaimed.

"No more than you wanting to go on a rescue mission without proper rest and in filthy clothes."

So that's what this was all about.

Iyon triumphantly shook his mane, satisfied that his point was made clear. By the end of their talk, they had reached Dahlia's cabin.

Dahlia was a kind and gentle widow. For the most part, she lived alone in a cabin larger than most in the valley. She was deemed with special permission to live in such a place, despite the fact that the cabins were meant for large families and those willing to work on the land. She tediously worked on an extraordinarily large garden that needed her constant tending, but with the purpose of producing the rarest of herbs and plants needed for human survival. She was a petite, dark-skinned woman, with a passion to help those who were suffering. Her entire family had been lost when her town was invaded by the Skeign. Since the day she had found refuge in Tolare, she'd made it her mission to help those in need and to find homes for the orphaned children who were brought to the city. Most importantly, Dahlia had the amazing ability to heal the sick and wounded through the use of her herbs and special plants. News of this spread quickly through the city and, in time, her cabin became known as the healing home of Tolare.

Dahlia was working in her garden when she heard the sound of hooves approaching. She could tell immediately by the steady and powerful gait that it was Iyon. Grabbing her hair wrap from the inside pocket of her work tunic, she pulled and tied her long, ebony hair, now streaked with grey, behind her head. She came around to the front of her home and saw Iyon approaching with Jen on his back.

The elder clasped her hands together at the sight of Jen, with a smile that went from cheek to cheek.

Just when Jen thought she was going to get one of those famous grandmother-like greetings, Dahlia's calm poise surprised her. Dahlia approached them and after giving Iyon a pat on the neck, she took Jen's hand and helped her down and into the cabin.

Iyon whispered to the elder, "I'll be by before sunrise for her."

Dahlia looked at her dear friend and nodded, then walked Jen inside her cabin.

Jen looked over her shoulder and said half-mockingly, "Good night, Iyon."

Iyon looked toward the spunky teenager and replied, "Good night, young Hanning."

The night for Jen was unusually quiet but came with the most amazing food she had ever tasted and a special tunic fashioned for adventure and made from the best material in all of Tolare.

By night's end, Jen was led to a room off the main floor that was full of books, journals, maps, and scrolls. With a gentle smile, Dahlia looked into the room. "This is your father's room. I know he would want you to sleep in here tonight. Fear not what tomorrow brings. I know full well you will be able to bring him home."

With that, the elder left Jen to settle down, climbed the stairs that led to the upper room and gently closed the door to her bedroom.

Jen took a short look around at everything her father had been working on and grunted, "Hmm, impressive. Looks like Tolare has brought another side of my dad out that I never knew."

Feeling proud, Jen lay on the soft bed and being at more peace than she had in months, Jen drifted off into a deep sleep.

Chapter 10
Shadow Earth

Jen was woken by the nudge of a huge nostril in her face. Completely disoriented, she rolled over and fell off the bed.

Iyon neighed softly as he heard the sound of sighing on the other side of the bed.

"Good morning, Jen. Are you awake?"

Jen pulled herself off the floor and stood up facing Iyon with her arms crossed. Iyon looked dumbly back at her.

"What is the matter? That is exactly how I have to wake your father up, except he doesn't fall out of the bed as you do. Very interesting custom you have."

Jen could only laugh. "I'm not as bad as my father. I usually beat the sun and run in the morning. So next time, I'll be giving you the nudge."

"I highly doubt that. Hope is ready for our arrival so we must leave now."

"But I haven't eaten."

"She has something special for you, so come." Iyon turned to leave and pranced through the living room and out the front door.

Jen whispered her thoughts just to see if Iyon could hear again. "Does Dahlia mind large animals prancing through her home?"

As soon as she walked through the front door she was scooped up and Iyon leaped into the air. This time Jen grabbed the collar instantly and held on tight.

"Animal you say? Do I look like an animal to you?" With that, Iyon flew high into the sky. He whipped his tail valiantly, letting electricity flare from it, filling the early morning sky, and then flew as fast, yet elegantly around the bolts.

They landed at a temple. Jared and a small band of soldiers dressed for action lined up outside. Iyon knelt and let Jen slide off, then he walked with great and powerful strides to the very center of the temple, saying, "Can an animal do that?"

Jared looked up at a stunned Jen. "Animal, huh?"

"Yep."

"Knew it as soon as I saw the lightning trick. Not surprised, though. Your father made the same mistake."

"Right," she grunted.

With that, Jared and a few that were with him joined Iyon at the center as he pounded his hoof and the group was lowered into the dark abyss.

Hope wasted no time with morning pleasantries. As soon as the group was lowered into the abyss, her glow filled the cavern. As soon as they were level with the portal, Hope's light burned bright orange, and from within the light came a map that floated straight into Jen's hands. She unfolded it while Hope explained, "This is one of the latest maps your father sketched for us. The picture of the tall lifeless tree stump indicates the location of the only entrance to Shadow Earth. I'll come back to pick you up as soon as I know you're standing by the tree. Test your travel capabilities before going to any of the places that you see on the map. Stare at something nearby, close your eyes, picture it, and when you open your eyes, you should be at that location you pictured in your mind. And Jen, you won't be going alone."

Jen looked behind her and took notice again of the three soldiers with weapons sheathed at their sides and in their hands as well. Each man wore an emerald ring that at times reflected the light that came from Hope.

Hope spoke up. "These men will accompany you into Shadow Earth. They're well trained and will protect you. Follow their instructions as they have all worked by your father's side."

Hope stopped talking for a moment and gave the soldiers a chance to introduce themselves. The first one in line was very dark-skinned, of medium height, and built for war. He stepped forward, nodded his head and said, "I go by Fox and am the leader for this mission. We've evaded the enemy with your father and we will do so with you."

The next soldier, shorter and stockier, introduced himself as Jeremiah. The third one, the tallest of the three, was Azar. Jen nodded to them as they said their names.

"I have two more items to give you," Hope said. A tan linen bag floated to Jen. She opened the bag and found five pieces of fruit inside. Jen pulled one out and studied it. "It kind of looks like a mango."

"Years ago, Iyon's father collected the seeds from a place called Eshron and we now grow them here. One piece of this fruit, which we call birr, will keep you energized for up to two days."

Jen took a bite immediately. The fruit was indeed empowering. Just a few bites and she was full. Not being able to finish, she held the fruit in front of Iyon, expecting him to snatch up the yummy leftover morsel. Iyon eyed her and with one precise laser shot from his eye, the leftover morsel was eradicated. He leaned closer to her and politely said, "In the future, I will not be responsible for disposing of your leftovers. There are other ways we deal with that here."

Jen shook her head and chuckled, *guess he's really not a horse after all.*

As Jen held the bag, an emerald ring, similar to the ones the warriors wore, floated out of Hope's mysterious glow and headed straight to Jen. She held out her hand, palm down, and the ring fastened itself onto her ring finger, fitting perfectly. Holding her hand in front of her face, she marveled at the beauty of the ring.

"This ring will prevent the Skeign from detecting you and give you access to our safe houses. If the Skeign can sense you in Tranquil Earth, imagine how fast they'll detect you in their own home ground. Never take this ring off, Jen. Otherwise, they'll find you, and you'll have no place to hide." Hope's glow suddenly changed into a swirl of radiant colors.

Jen looked into the rainbow of light and asked, "Won't Iyon be coming with?"

"Iyon must stay here. His presence in Shadow Earth cannot be hidden. Even with the power of the gem, the Skeign would eventually detect him, and the mission would be jeopardized. It's time, Jen. The soldiers will proceed first, and then you'll follow," Hope said.

Fox and the others didn't hesitate. With weapons ready, they marched into the portal. Then Jen swung the sack of fruit over her shoulder, put the map in her pocket, and followed them.

As soon as they landed in Shadow Earth, Fox, Jeremiah, and Azar scattered in three different directions to survey the area. Jen stayed by the tree. The once glowing tree that had been their portal now looked lifeless. She leaned against it as she took in her surroundings. The only light was that of a blood-stained sun. The rugged terrain was devoid of vegetation. There were no shrubs or flowers to add a splash of color. The wind howled through the jagged crevices of the stone hills nearby. Shadow Earth was a land of absolute despair. Jen's eyes watered as the oppression of this horrible place bore down upon her.

Seeing Jen's reaction, Fox went to her. "Don't worry, Jen. All is clear. Are you ready to conduct your first test?"

"Yes, I'm ready," she said and brushed the feelings of emptiness aside.

"Then let's move a little further down into the valley. You can practice more safely there." Fox, Jeremiah, Azar, and Jen quickly descended into the valley until they reached a petrified tree stump. All four of them stood about fifty feet from it. Then the soldiers stepped back away from Jen. She looked at Fox hesitantly, but he nodded to her reassuringly. "You know what to do."

Jen nodded back. "Right." She stared at the stump.

Just like Hope said. What did she say? Picture the stump in my mind, close my eyes and open them.

Jen did so, and when she opened her eyes, she almost tripped over the stump that a moment ago had been about fifty feet away. The soldiers cheered in the distance.

Jen looked back at them and smiled broadly. *Now I'll be able to find Dad!* She closed her eyes and thought of Fox. When she opened them, she was standing in front of the soldiers again.

"Good job, Jen, but you need to practice more before we proceed with our mission," Fox said. Jen was anxious to find her dad and didn't want to spend more time practicing. But despite her impatience, she didn't want to argue with a man who was her father's comrade.

Over the next hour, Jen was made to disappear and reappear in a number of locations. Fox had her practice until she could transition herself to five different places in a matter of seconds. The soldiers were astonished at how quickly she learned all the ins and outs of teleportation. They knew that perfecting this skill was necessary in order for her to succeed.

Azar spoke up. "She is as gifted as her father is for this traveling. Let's not waste any more time. Let Jen lead us to John and the others."

Everyone agreed. They signaled Jen to come to them. She looked down at them from a two-hundred foot ledge.

Jeremiah spoke for the group. "Jen, we believe you're ready to carry out the mission. Pull out your map. I want to show you something."

Jen got the map from her back pocket and unfolded it.

Pointing to a rock that looked like a wheel in front of a mountain, Jeremiah said, "Picture this location in your mind exactly as you see it on the map and transport yourself there. Press your hand with the ring against that rock and it'll roll away, revealing the entrance to one of our safe houses. As soon as you go in, the rock will roll back in place. The emerald ring will trigger the lantern inside to light up. Memorize the room, or something significant in the room, picture one of us and then return. Do you understand these directions?"

"Yes, I'll be back in a couple of minutes." She closed her eyes and was gone and the soldiers started their journey on foot to the safe house.

Chapter 11
Close Encounter

When Jen opened her eyes, she was standing at the foot of a mountain. Several large rocks lay nearby. She scanned the area to look for enemies, but all she saw was badlands, no movement of any kind. Not even the wind dared to breathe. She searched the mountain's base until she saw the giant wheel-shaped boulder that Jeremiah had indicated on the map. She ran over to it and pressed her ring against it. The rock pivoted and slowly rolled out, revealing a narrow opening to the safe house. Once she was inside, the rock rolled back in place, concealing the entrance. But Jen wasn't left in the dark. A lantern, positioned on a plain circular stone table, lit up the chamber that was somewhat bigger than her living room. She walked over to it and set the bag she received from Hope down on it as she looked around. Five small cots sat in a row against one wall. Along another wall were several sealed boxes labeled Ammunition, Packaged Food, and Bottled Water. Jen did her best to memorize the details of the room, but she felt it was plain enough to recall. After glancing around one last time, she stepped back to get a full view of the room. Then, picturing Fox in her mind, she disappeared.

When Jen reappeared, Fox immediately put his hand over mouth and pulled her down behind the rocks where he and the other soldiers were hiding. Jen made a muffled noise, but the others held their fingers to their mouths, pleading with her to be silent. Once Jen realized the imminent danger, she nodded. Fox slowly released his hand to uncover her mouth. Jen barely breathed as she stared into the other soldiers' eyes and saw their fear. Azar looked at her and mouthed, "Skeign." Jen crouched as low as she could behind the fallen rocks and listened in horror to the thumping of the monstrous paws and the scraping of the sharp claws against the rocky ground as the Skeign drew closer.

"How did they find us?" Jen mouthed and then pointed to the ring.

"I don't know. Something's wrong," Fox expressed in silence.

With no place to go, Jen and the soldiers were trapped. Fox leaned over to Jen and articulated slowly, "If they get too close, leave and continue the mission without us. We'll fight our way out. Go to the safe room." Fox moved away from her and motioned to his men to be ready to fight.

There has to be another way! Then Jen had a dangerous idea. She could create a diversion in hopes that the Skeign would move away from the others. She looked at Azar, his arms locked around his weapon, and she held up her hand, signaling him to wait. The sound of the enemy's thick, heavy breathing drew nearer. She closed her eyes and vanished.

Upon opening her eyes, Jen found herself lying on her stomach, staring at the Skeign from the top of a rock hill. She counted three beasts spread out, looking about the rocks. One of them was steadily approaching her comrades. Jen made her move. She threw down a rock and then disappeared, reappearing in an instant on the opposite side of the valley where boulders hid her. Just then, the Skeign leaped toward the fallen rock.

I have to keep them moving away or they'll see the others!

With no time to think, Jen doubled back, moving herself closer to the lifeless tree where they'd entered Shadow Earth. Jen kicked and threw rocks, anything to make noise, and then disappeared as fast as she could. She worked herself closer to the portal, but stayed shy of it by almost thirty yards.

Jen was lying in the dirt with little coverage, shocked at how exhausted she'd become due to traveling in this way. The Skeign's roaring signaled their fast approach. Jen's breathing quickened, and her whole body trembled. One of the Skeign spotted her. It took to the air, and was coming straight for her. Her vision blurred and her breathing began to race. She couldn't drag her thoughts to the present; they were jumbled and incoherent. The creature of death was almost upon her, its nostrils flaring and mouth open, ready to capture its prey. At the final second, Jen recalled the wheel-shaped rock and vanished, leaving the dismayed monster to claw at nothing but the ground before it.

Once again, Jen was standing in front of the rock and breathed a sigh of relief. She extended her arms and shook out her hands, feeling the calm return to her. She was about to enter the safe house and wait for the others, but then stopped short. She took a few deep breaths to regain her strength and decided to look for her dad by herself.

Jen closed her eyes and recalled the last dinner she'd had with her parents. Her dad was sitting there, so content and full of life, with her mom seated across the table from him. Feeling that her memory was solid, Jen opened her eyes. She found herself at the entrance of a dark and gloomy cave at the foot of a giant mountain.

"Dad?" she called out. Again, Jen felt confused and woozy from her travel.

From out of the blackness of the cave came the voice of something other than her father. It was the sound of a gentle wind that blew out and caressed her face with a strange kind of peace. It danced around her as it attempted to soothe her anxiety.

"You are tired," sang the wind. "Come in and find rest."

Jen hesitated at first, but the wind continued its dance. Jen closed her eyes as the wind danced around her, making her mind cloudy and eventually blank. Seizing the opportunity, the wind invaded her as she inhaled it and then it cast its spell on her.

I could use a rest. She entered the dark cave. All thoughts of travel dissipated as the wind continued to control her mind, and enticed her to rest, and so she decided to lie down. She soon fell into a deep sleep. After a while, the gentleness of the wind changed. It hissed and snarled, but Jen was fast asleep. Knowing full well that its prey was vulnerable, the beast emerged from the depths of the cave. The Skeign panted hungrily as it leaned over Jen. Its drool dripped on her clothes. Then, with its iron tentacles, the predator picked up its unsuspecting victim and withdrew into its lair.

....

Jen woke up to total darkness. She tried to move but couldn't, for she was bolted to a dungeon wall with iron cuffs about her feet, hands, and neck. She was completely disoriented and could not remember where she was and how she'd ended up bolted to a wall. But worse than that, she could not recall even who she was.

"No!" gasped Jen as she shook the bonds holding her firmly in place. But it was useless. The iron cuffs bound her mercilessly to the wall. Tears streamed down her face as the gravity of her situation sank in.

"Hello?" cried a man's voice, so hoarse it barely sounded like a man at all. "You finally awake? Please, answer me. Don't be afraid," he called again, this time more desperately.

Flushed with relief that she wasn't alone, Jen called out into the darkness, "I'm scared."

The man laughed. "So am I."

"Where are we?" she asked, this time a little louder.

"We're in the torture chambers of the Skeign. There's no track of time down here, only pain and misery."

The man's words made Jen's blood run cold. In pity of what was about to happen to her, she whimpered, "I can't remember anything. Why I'm here or who I am. How long have I been out?"

"I can answer one part. When they brought you down and locked you up, there were three of us here who have been bolted to these walls for what seems like weeks. But after you came, about each day they have taken one of my comrades out. Now there is only me. So that means you've been here maybe two days. And you sound a bit young too? How old are you?"

"Too young to be here."

After a moment of silence, the man said in stunned amazement, "You're the girl, aren't you? You're John's daughter!" he ended, laughing in surprise.

The man's words were what Jen needed to jog her memory back, and it was working.

"Yes. I'm Jen, John's daughter. You're one of his comrades, aren't you?" Finally, it was all coming back now.

"Yes ma'am, at your service. Name's Habin, and you need to find John before it's too late for him."

Jen almost whimpered but sucked it up and got her words out. "I have to get to my father. Habin, I travel as he does, but when I thought of him, it didn't work and I ended up here instead. I don't know what I'm supposed to do."

"Wait a minute…" Just then, ghastly shrieks were heard. They lasted for a few seconds and then they mutated into horrifying animal-like growls.

"That was Chase, my comrade!" Habin cried in remorse at the loss of another friend. He fought hard to speak out words despite what he was feeling.

"They are coming for you next, I know it. Listen to me, Jen! Listen to me. If you don't leave, they'll strip you of your mind…your will…emotions…." Habin's voice began to trail off as he spoke.

"Habin! Stay with me! Habin!"

By this point, the valiant soldier's defenses had almost broken down, for the power of evil was attacking his mind in every way. Habin realized he was losing his ability to speak freely. With every bit of strength he had left, he spoke urgently to Jen. "Rid your mind of this place. Think not of your father, but picture a…golden…three-pronged…key…tied to his…hand. Hurry!" Habin stopped speaking words but made groaning sounds instead. The enemy had succeeded in muting him.

The dungeon door flew open with a resounding bang. A red ray radiating from the Skeign's eyes shot through the room, providing enough light for Jen to see Habin. He was bound to the wall as she was. His clothes were badly torn, and his head tilted listlessly against the iron collar. He was nothing but skin and bones. The glimpse lasted only a second as she turned her attention back to the creature slowly stomping toward her. The Skeign predator callously said, "My Master desires you now. I will be honored in front of all and your soul will belong to him!"

A long, thin metallic tentacle reached up and stung Jen on the back side of her neck. She screamed in agony as a bolt of electricity shot from her neck and traveled down her spine, then spread throughout the rest of her body. She desperately fought for control to block out the pain. Jen knew that she must focus, or she would surely die. She took Habin's advice and pictured a beautiful golden key with three prongs tied to her dad's hand. As the Skeign was about to rip Jen's body from the wall, she vanished. It roared horribly in defeat. In its anger, the creature turned to its other prisoner, slashed the restraints off the wall, and dragged him out of the room. "I will make you pay for her escape!"

The soldier could make no facial expression as he was being led away. Though he knew he wouldn't live to see the final outcome of the war, the hope of victory once again flooded his soul. Deep inside, Habin smiled.

Chapter 12
Reunited

Jen opened her eyes. She was standing in an underground cave lit by a single torch attached to a pillar. She briefly looked around this dismal place. Off to her left was what appeared to be the only exit, but it had been barricaded by a mass of rocks and huge boulders. The noise of digging and screeching could be faintly heard from somewhere far above. She crept around the pillars, frantically searching for him. Turning to the right, she let out a gasp, for there, lying on the ground next to a wall, was her father!

"Dad!" Jen ran to him and knelt, cradling his head in her arms. His clothes were ripped, and his arms, legs and face were covered in dirt. Jen's cheeks were streaked with tears. Putting her fingers on her father's neck, she checked for a pulse and felt it still beating strong. "Dad, wake up! Please, wake up!" No response. Jen gently set his head back down and whispered in his ear, "I promise you, I'll be right back." With that, Jen vanished.

....

Fox and the others were inside the safe house, discussing how to find Jen, when she suddenly appeared in their midst.

"Jen, you're back!" Fox jumped up and bear hugged her, then he looked her square in the eyes and yelled, "You better never do a fool thing like that again! You need to learn about chain of command."

"But Fox, I found my dad! He's unconscious, and I can't get him to wake up. I can hear the Skeign digging from above. The ceiling is gonna come crashing down any minute! What do I do?"

"Here!" called Azar, "Give him this." He reached down and picked up the linen bag filled with birrs and yanked one out. He also pulled out his pocket knife.

"Cut through this birr and let the juice trickle into his mouth. Keep that up, and he will wake up. Come back here as soon as you can with him."

Jen took the piece of fruit and the knife from Azar and stepped back. "I'll return as fast as I can." Before the soldiers could nod their heads, she was gone.

....

Jen reappeared right next to her father. The pounding continued above, causing dust and bits of debris to fall from the ceiling. Jen knelt down and placed John's head in her lap. She took the knife, stabbed the fruit and held it above his mouth, making sure the juice trickled into his mouth. A minute seemed like an eternity for Jen as she waited for any sort of response from him. Finally, John's eyes squinted and popped open. His body tensed and he screamed, "No!!"

"Dad! It's me, Jen! I'm right here."

For a moment, John's eyes were wild and he was unresponsive to her, but she continued to talk to him, hoping that the sound of her voice would bring him back.

After a minute, John became more alert, and he sat up and finally noticed who was there with him. "Am I still dreaming?"

"No, Dad, it's really me," she said with a sincere smile. "Hope found me and sent me to find you. I'm here with you right now."

For a moment in time, he bear hugged his daughter, wept and kissed her forehead and cheek. "Is your mother here too?"

"No, I don't know where she is. But don't worry, Dad. Hope is looking for her."

Jen tried to hold back her tears as she gazed into her father's face, but it was impossible. His eyes were bloodshot. She tenderly took his hand and saw that a key on a chain had been tied to it.

"I was unconscious. You shouldn't have been able to find me. How on Earth did you know where I was?"

"I ran into Habin inside a dungeon. He told me to picture the key in your hand. It brought me straight to you."

John cocked his head, shocked at that comment. "A dungeon? Did Habin escape with you?"

Jen shook her head. "I'm sorry, Dad. I know he was your friend."

John didn't respond right away. Then with a heavy heart, he said, "Yes, he was. There's a lot I need to tell you, but first, we have to get out of here."

The vibrations intensified and the whole room was shaking now. Pebbles and rocks were falling from the ceiling.

"The Skeign is looking everywhere for this," he said, holding up his hand with the key.

"I know the hideout you have. It's small with five cots in a row and it has a lantern in the center. Do you know that one?"

"Know it? I fixed it up."

"Are you strong enough to travel?"

"Not sure," John said, which worried Jen.

"I'm right here, Dad, I'm with you and I'm not leaving without you. I've been looking for you with the help of Fox, Azar, and Jeremiah. Let's think of them so we can go where they are. Then we'll be safe."

John sighed. Something was obviously bothering him.

"Okay, let's go."

He put his arm around his daughter. The roaring above them continued as more debris fell all over the room. The ceiling itself was beginning to cave in.

John and Jen thought of their mutual friends and disappeared.

Chapter 13
Safe House?

"Jen, John, you made it!" Fox cheered as he bounded to his feet, along with the others.

"It's good to see you, too," John replied, while clasping their hands.

Fox signaled Azar and Jeremiah to get food and water, but the two were already working on it. Fox looked down and saw what was in John's hand, his child-like trance expressing his wonder. "Of all the great things to witness in a lifetime," Fox chuckled. "John, do you know what that is?"

"I studied your history. I know the importance of it," he stated triumphantly.

Food was brought to him and Jen. As they ate, Jen took in her father's demeanor. His hands were shaking as he gulped down the water and savagely devoured the birr fruit. His eyes couldn't keep still as he continually glanced around the room like he was expecting some sort of an ambush. Jen had never seen him like this before. Had the war affected him so badly, or was it something else? John finished off the last of the birr, took a few sips of water and then abruptly stood up.

"Okay, it's time for me to go."

Fox stood up, seemingly confused by the rapid change in his comrade's behavior. "John, it's okay, we're safe here. The Skeign haven't found this place before. They're not going to now."

Looking at Fox, John slammed his fist on the table and yelled, "Yes, they will, Fox!" John exploded. He didn't mean to snap. But he could feel pressure building all around him. "I'm sorry, man. Somehow they found a way to infiltrate my mind. I didn't want to picture any of our safe houses for fear they would follow me there. I separated myself from my men and knew of a place that the complete entrance and path had caved in, but the safe haven on the inside was still intact. So I took a sedative because while I'm asleep, I'm untraceable. Then the next thing I remember is Jen waking me up."

John looked at the key in his hand. "Those men risked their lives for this." Overcome with anguish, he paused for a moment to try and collect himself. The room was silent. Then he went on, "The Skeign are coming. I'm sorry, Fox. Even though I have the ring, they still found a way to track me down. It's not immediate but it's true. I don't know what's going on, but if I don't leave now, they'll find us all, and you three can't escape like Jen and I."

John pulled a knife from his leg pocket and cut the cord that bound the key to his hand. Then he turned and placed the key and its chain in Jen's palm and closed her fingers around them.

"Get this to Hope, Jen. I'll get myself to the portal. Do not come after me. You must listen to me," John said firmly, then brought her close to him and hugged her tight, "I love you. Don't forget that." With a kiss on the forehead, he vanished.

"Dad!" Jen screamed.

"Don't do it, Jen!" Fox pleaded.

Jen moved a step away from Fox, wanting so badly to go after her dad. To lose him again after all this time was unbearable.

"Jen, are you with us?" Fox asked.

Jen nodded. She took the key and chain and stuffed them in her pants pocket.

"We have to go. Let's gather every Taser we can hold," Fox said. Within minutes, all the soldiers had Tasers in their hands. They also had other weapons that resembled rifles strapped behind their backs. Then Fox called to his team, "Let's move out."

The four of them struck out and trekked across the mountains and through the valleys. Jen traveled ahead of the others, checking out the terrain. Whenever she saw a Skeign, she returned to the soldiers and took them through a path that was safe. When night fell, they cleverly hid in small crevices that went deep into the earth, too small for any Skeign to find. The following day they continued their treacherous journey back to the dead tree that was finally only a few short hundred yards away.

"I'll go to the portal first to alert Hope. I'll signal you when it's safe to come." Without waiting for a response, Jen disappeared.

She stood before the lifeless tree and waited. The thought of leaving her dad behind weighed heavily upon her. Then she heard something like a sonic boom. Jen looked behind her and saw the three soldiers running like mad toward her, and behind them was a massive vortex spinning in the valley. The trunk of the tree began to spread. They were moments away from leaving Shadow Earth.

I'll just take a few seconds to find Dad and tell him we're leaving. I'm doing it!

"Jen!" yelled the others, but it was too late.

Normally, the journey of the thought lasted only a second, but something bizarre happened this time. Jen felt as if she was flying, and everything was a blur.

"Jen, I told you not to come after me."

"What's going on?"

"I'm transitioning so fast to confuse them. Stop following me. Go back to the tree."

"Not without you."

"Fine, since this has put your life in danger, I'll go back with you."

In a matter of seconds, Jen and John found themselves back with the others, standing by the tree. The portal was opening. Fox, who was out of breath, handed John a Taser. Then turning to Jen, Fox said in frustration, "Man, Jennifer, you have to stop doing that to us."

"Yes, sir."

Just as the portal opened, something long and slithery slashed at Hope, igniting the portal entrance with a strange poison. Fox and the others turned and behind them was an uncanny Skeign, unlike the others. This one was much smaller and the color of the rocks. It had the head of a serpent with a tongue full of poison.

"Kill it!" yelled John.

Fox and the others opened fire, destroying the beast, but not before the damage was done. They looked toward the vortex in the valley and saw hundreds of Skeign pouring from it.

"What just happened?" yelled Jen as she looked at Hope, who had turned a sickly green color.

"I'm okay, but the portal, it's stuck. I won't be able to close it," admitted Hope. "Not from my end."

"Jen, jump, we'll follow," John commanded.

"We go together!" Jen demanded.

John gave Fox a quick eye which gave him an unspoken command to follow. Fox and the others seized Jen and jumped through the portal, leaving John behind. Snarling and screeching, the entire Skeign army swarmed to the entrance, ready to finally invade Tolare. Without a second to spare, John blasted the entire tree with all the fire power he had on him. The dead tree exploded, fragments flying high into the sky, destroying the portal to Tolare. John leaped as he fired and landed behind a few small rocks to take refuge from the explosion.

He could've disappeared instantly, but he didn't. He had just destroyed the only known way of entering and leaving Shadow Earth. He'd trapped himself there. But if he hadn't, all of Tolare would have been under attack. With a renewed sense of strength and hope now that the key was with Jen, he turned around and courageously faced the deadly army of the Skeign. Felonious, the ruthless commander of Shadow Earth and also a dragon, stepped forward and opened his mouth. His two-pronged snakelike tongue slithered out toward John. John fearlessly stared into his enemy's eyes, grinned, and said, "You mindless beast. I won't go down that easily. Try and get this if you want it so badly." John hid an object in his fist and then vanished.

Felonious stood there for a while in front of his legion and waited patiently, knowing he would eventually find John again. The fact that John had no clue as to its new method of tracking him gave this creature great delight. Felonious would find John and the key; it was only a matter of time. Failure meant torture from the Master and that thought was not something Felonious would accept.

After patiently waiting, John's presence was sensed. "Ah, there you are," the beast said. The chase was on!

Chapter 14
Back to Dahlia's House

Jen flew out the other side of the portal, with Fox and Jeremiah still holding on to her and Azar right behind them. The floating stone softened like a mattress, cushioning their fall. As they struggled to their feet, the platform immediately hardened again, and quickly rose to the top until they were safely above ground. Jared and Iyon were there waiting.

"Let me go! I have to go back!" Jen screamed. She punched Fox in the jaw, probably hurting herself more than she did him. Startled by the punch, Fox released Jen's arm.

Jared jumped toward her and tried to bear hug her until she calmed down.

"Jen, it's okay, it's okay," was all Jared could say. She ignored him and jerked around to look for her dad, but he had not followed them through the portal. Panic-stricken, Jen screamed at them, "No! No! Bring him back! Bring him back now!"

Jen relentlessly fought to be free from Jared's hold. Fox and the others stood by sadly, for they all knew that nothing could be done for John now.

"I'm sorry, Jen. I'm so sorry," Jared said sympathetically. Then turning to Fox he asked, "What happened?"

"Just as we were about to leave Shadow Earth, a Skeign snuck up on us and did something to the portal. It was stuck, so after we went through, John stayed behind to destroy the portal. He stopped the invasion."

Jen stopped fighting with Jared as the full impact of Fox's words hit her. She buried her head in Jared's chest and wept bitterly.

Jared was no stranger to this kind of grief. He knew so many whose loved ones had been captured or killed by the enemy. How many more would they have to lose before the war would end? He was relieved when Jen finally stopped crying, but his relief changed to concern when he noticed she had become too quiet in his arms.

Energy rapidly drained from Jen's body. With what little strength she had left, Jen reached in her pocket and pulled out the key. She looked at it for a second. It fell out of her hand as she began to lose consciousness. One of the last things she heard was its resounding clink on the temple floor. The guards standing nearby stared at it in amazement and disbelief. If that was the same key that had been stolen from them so long ago, then there was still hope of winning this war.

"Jen, Jen!" Jared said. Jen's body sagged in his arms. Her head leaned off to one side, and that's when he saw it.

"Oh no," he said under his breath and looked up desperately at Iyon.

Jared pointed to the cursed mark of the Skeign on the side of Jen's neck. Iyon took a moment to glance at the wound and his ears flattened to his head. "They poisoned her! Put her on my back!"

In a matter of seconds, Jen was lying on his back. The gem on Iyon's collar slightly glowed, its power keeping Jen safely in place as Iyon tore into the sky, racing for Dahlia's home. Jared stayed behind with the others to organize a set of troops to watch over the key until Jen's safe return.

Dahlia was busy working in her garden as usual when she heard the sound of horrendous neighing that came from the air above. She knew exactly what that meant. A sense of urgency rushed through her as she feared the worst. She grabbed her hair tie from the inside pocket of her work tunic, pulled and tied her hair back as she was running toward the front of the house. As soon as he landed, Dahlia saw the young woman draped across his back. Dahlia looked up at Iyon as if reading his mind.

"Not your fault, Iyon. Do not blame yourself," Dahlia said.

He ignored her statement. "She was stung by the Skeign. The poison took effect as soon as she returned from Shadow Earth."

"Come," said Dahlia as she went quickly inside, knowing full well any chance of recovery would depend on a miracle. Jen was carried in and placed on a soft feather bed. She was sweating profusely.

Iyon stood over Jen on one side of the bed while Dahlia sat on the other side, dabbing her forehead with a wet towel. Dahlia set the towel aside and gently opened Jen's eyes to study them, and then looked up apprehensively at Iyon.

"Medicines alone won't wake her up. The poison has invaded her physical body, and her mind is in the world of Escapist now. She is trapped in her subconscious mind and that's where they plan to get to her. As long as she is there, she won't remember here."

"John is trapped in Shadow Earth and Jen is trapped in Escapist. Jen is John's only chance of being rescued." Iyon bent his head down and gently let his nose rub against Jen's cheek. "I know what I must try and do. Go make the remedy and give it to her no matter what you see me doing here. Stop for nothing."

Without saying anything else, Dahlia rose, went into the kitchen, and began gathering the necessary supplies to help clear the toxins from Jen's body. After she left the room, Iyon's eyes turned a royal blue. Rays extended from his eyes and gently penetrated Jen down to her soul. This gave him entrance into the dream realm where he would search for Jen. Not only was it a fight for her life, it was a race against time to save her father too, before it would be too late for him.

Chapter 15
Into the World of Escapist

"Jen, baby, it's time to wake up. You'll be late for school."

Jen's head whirled in pain. She opened her eyes and found herself lying in her bed back at home, and there was her mother, putting folded socks in her dresser drawer across from her bed.

"Hurry up and get dressed so you can come eat breakfast with us."

With a peaceful smile that lit up her whole face, Adriana looked down at her daughter and then left the room.

Us?

Jen slipped out of bed and darted into the kitchen where she saw her father eating eggs and toast in his usual spot at the table. He was dressed for work in his usual lab uniform. Adriana was leaning against the counter as she drank her morning coffee. Jen stared at them as if she were seeing two ghosts. John stopped eating for a moment and looked up at his bewildered daughter.

"Honey, is something the matter?" John casually asked. "Did you have any strange dreams last night?"

Before Jen could answer him, Adriana budded in, "Maybe she should go to the doctor again. Ever since she bumped her head, she hasn't been the same."

"Hmm, maybe you're right," John said.

"No," Jen said quickly. "Mom, Dad, really, I'm fine. It's just—I forgot what day it was, that's all."

Adriana looked at her daughter and chuckled. "Too many late nights for you. Well, it's Monday, and you probably forgot because you don't want to take that history test today. Get ready or you'll be late for school. Oh, Jen, are you sure you didn't have any peculiar dreams last night?"

Jen looked quizzically at her mother, unsure how to answer her. "No, nothing out of the ordinary." She went to her room and looked around. Everything appeared to be normal.

I guess I must have hit my head pretty hard because I can't remember anything this morning. Jen shrugged her shoulders and after getting ready, she hurried off to school.

As she walked to her first class, she saw Lynette and her sidekicks coming toward her. A sense of dread came over Jen as Lynette approached.

"Hey, Jen," said Lynette, smiling. "Great run at the last meet. Do you think you'll be ready in time to compete against our arch rivals from Hiansville? I know the accident wasn't too long ago, but we sure could use you."

Shocked, Jen almost stuttered, "Umm, don't worry, Lynette, I'll be ready. I wouldn't miss it for anything. See you later."

Jen walked away, smiling. *Is this real? But why would I expect something else?*

"See ya," Lynette called back.

After a few days, Jen became acclimated to this dream world. She participated in cross-country and excelled at it. She helped the Drama Club build their set for the next big performance, and every now and then they would joke about the day she fell off the ladder and bumped her head on the dungeon wall. This was now her reality.

After supper one evening, John and Adriana decided to go for a stroll.

"Be back in a bit," Adriana called as she took John's hand and dragged him out the door.

Jen laughed at them. Her father was like putty in her mother's hands. She cleaned up the kitchen, grabbed the garbage bag, and carried it out back. Opening the door, she stopped dead in her tracks. There before her was a beautiful white stallion grazing in her backyard.

"No way!" she exclaimed.

Jen cautiously approached Iyon. "Hey there, I'm not going to hurt you." She reached up and stroked his neck, filled with childlike wonder at this amazing encounter.

Iyon gazed deep into Jen's eyes, looking to see if he could find the girl within that knew him. Sadly, he could tell that she had no clue she was living in a fantasy world. He rubbed his forehead against her stomach, making Jen laugh. Little did she know that was all Iyon needed to do in order to gently interject his power into her and take her home.

"What are you doing, boy?"

Iyon suddenly sensed a sinister presence that prevented him from transferring his power into her and taking her home. Something strong and inexplicable was blocking him. His plan had failed.

The front door opened, and John and Adriana entered the house.

"Jen, we're home. Where are you?"

Not wanting to be seen by anyone else, Iyon quickly dashed into the woods. Jen stood there, staring into the forest.

"Jen, Jen," her mother kept calling.

"I'm taking out the garbage. Be right in." After Jen finished, she went in for the night. She rarely kept secrets from her parents, but for some reason, she wanted to keep this one to herself.

Iyon ran through the forest, angry that he had missed a perfect opportunity. Now he would have to wait patiently for another chance and figure out why his first plan didn't work.

The next day was Saturday, and Jen was preparing for a morning jog. Adriana was cooking breakfast when she noticed Jen getting ready to leave. She wiped her hands on her apron and walked over to her.

"Where are you going so early?"

"Mom, come on. You know I like to jog on Saturdays."

"Well, since your accident you haven't. I want you back in fifteen minutes. There are some things the doctor said we need to go over today."

Jen sighed while finishing with her laces. "Mom, I'm in cross-country. A fifteen minute run is like a warm-up." She ran out the door.

"Fifteen or you're grounded."

"Okay, okay." She rose her hands in surrender as she ran off.

Jen jogged through her neighborhood and headed toward the school, not having any intention of making this a fifteen minute jog. She knew the courtyard would be empty and she had an overwhelming urge to go to the garden. When she got there, she took a minute and breathed in the sweet aroma of the flowers. After looking around to make sure no one else was there, she darted through the paths that led to the gazebo and the fountain.

When Jen reached the fountain, she held her hands under the flowing water and splashed some on her face. It felt refreshing after her run. Then she bent down to get a drink, but stopped short when she noticed a bizarre sight. In place of her reflection, Jen saw an entire village of people, their faces full of sorrow. And they seemed to be staring at her. Jen jumped away as the image made her recall similar ones. She fell to her knees. The wind blew through the flowers in a strange, yet familiar way. She buried her face in her hands as fragments of scary memories invaded her mind. "No, no, no!" She opened her eyes, hoping it would all be gone, but instead, the petals of the flowers surrounding the fountain turned black. She screamed, bolted to her feet and ran out of the garden. Outside, she came to a dead halt. The grass all around her became black, the leaves on the trees turned black. Strange memories flooded her mind, none of them making any sense. It was as if an explosion had gone off in her head as images swirled in her mind. The pain and the pressure were too much to bear. She grabbed her head, screamed and fell to the floor, losing consciousness.

Iyon, who had been following her from a distance in the woods, heard her scream and bolted toward her. He didn't know what had happened to her. He was about to enter the school's courtyard and had decided he would just pick her up, but was interrupted by the slamming of a car door and the yelling of her frantic mother, Adriana. With her was another person, whose presence exuded evil. Iyon found cover fast. If his cover was blown, they would guard Jen so heavily that he would never have a chance to rescue her. He darted behind one of the school's sheds and remained there until it was safe to leave.

Adriana, suspecting that her daughter hadn't listened, had gotten in her car, picked up one of the doctor's assistants who she was instructed to call on immediately if her daughter was acting strange or disobedient, and the two went in search of her. As she was driving down the road by the school, they both heard the screams. Slamming on her brakes, Adriana and the assistant jumped out of the car and ran down the path to the garden. There they saw Jen lying on the ground unconscious.

"I knew this would happen," exclaimed Adriana.

The man with her pulled a syringe out of his pocket, kneeled next to her and administered the shot into her forearm. Then he picked Jen up and carried her to the car while barking orders to Adriana.

"Take me straight to the hospital, ma'am. It's time we get this one some help. This other method isn't working, and that sedative will keep her knocked out until she is safe."

Iyon waited until they got into the car and drove off, then headed for the woods. He'd follow them safely to their destination. The discouragement of another missed opportunity raged inside him.

Chapter 16
Decision Time

It was Adriana's idea. John thought putting Jen in Elmwood Sanitarium was absurd, but Adriana's strong and stubborn will quickly crushed her husband's gentle spirit. After being admitted, Jen was still asleep from the sedative and settled into a private room. Her parents were in Dr. Brainier's office, discussing what should be done with her.

"Well, I do agree with your wife's concerns, Mr. Hanning. We tried it your way, to see if you could get her to explain the hallucinations. It didn't work. Jen is going to need more aggressive therapy to eliminate those. We'll start immediately. After a couple of weeks, when she is back under control, she can go home. To ignore this problem would be parental negligence, and I might be compelled to report it, sir. Do you understand what I'm saying?"

John sat there like a child in time-out. His wife's eyes were eating him alive with the expected answer, and the doctor was staring at him as if he were a shameful criminal. John responded apologetically. "Of course, I understand what you're saying, Dr. Brainier. I just felt it was a bit extreme to keep her locked up here. I mean, don't you think she should be resting at home?"

"John, I don't understand how you can say that," Adriana interjected. "We were advised to keep a careful eye on everything Jen did and said. I know she's had dreams, but she won't open up to me about them. She's already showing signs of deception. And why did she scream in the school courtyard? What did she see there, John? We're just not able to control her anymore. It's time to get answers. This is the right thing to do, the safest thing to do." Then, turning to Dr. Brainier, Adriana said, "Since the papers were already signed from the last time she was here, do you need anything else from us, Doctor?"

"Absolutely not, Mrs. Hanning, and it was right of you to call on our assistant and bring her here. Trust me, we'll get to the bottom of these dreams and cure your daughter. Good day to you."

The two got up to leave.

"Oh and one more thing; thank you for bringing her to us the first time. Getting her in our system was a crucial step and we are so relieved that you found her for us...silly me; I meant found your way to our facility for help. Well, good day to you now."

John and Adriana weren't allowed to say goodbye to Jen. Instead, nurses came in and ushered them out of the hospital, locking the doors behind them.

....

Surrounded by greenery and park benches to make it appear less threatening, Elmwood Sanitarium was an imposing structure, covering an entire city block. Iyon shuddered at the thought of Jen being in that place. He stood in the woods and watched the hospital doors, hoping to see Jen walk out with her parents. He knew that if they decided to leave her there, she would not make it out alive.

Iyon's worst fears were coming to pass. The doors opened and out came John and Adriana without Jen. They argued on the way back to their car, got in and drove off. Iyon had never been more disappointed in himself. *I should've seen this coming.* It was impossible for Iyon to get to Jen now. He couldn't risk being seen, for there was no way of telling where Escapist was lurking. Escapist was the dragon that controlled this artificial world. If she discovered Iyon trying to rescue Jen and called for reinforcements, then Jen's life would be taken before Iyon could safely rescue her. Refusing to take that kind of chance, he closed his eyes and disappeared. Another plan was needed.

....

As soon as Jen's parents were out of his hair, Dr. Brainier wrote out an order for his new patient and called for a nurse to come pick it up. Zurina entered the room and smiled amiably at the doctor.

"Yes, Dr. Brainier," she said cheerfully. Dr. Brainier looked at her and stared for a moment into her dark brown eyes. Though she wasn't the most professional member of his staff, she was definitely the most radiant. Her playful courtesy made her even more attractive. Maybe it was the smile or the way she batted her eyes at him whenever she leaned against his desk that he took as a sign of her affection. It wasn't long after she started working at the hospital that Dr. Brainier had fallen head over heels for the lovely Zurina.

He handed her the order. She took it from him, looked at it questioningly, and then said, "I'm sorry, Doctor, but I haven't seen this treatment used on teenagers before."

Dr. Brainier spoke authoritatively to her. "Zurina, I'll handle my little schizophrenic patient as I see fit, understood? Besides, this is no ordinary girl."

"Yes, sir. Sorry, sir," she responded rather playfully.

"Carry on, and please don't question my decisions again."

Zurina let her hands rest confidently on her hips and mischievously chided him. "You know you don't have to play tough doctor with me. There's no one here in the room that you need to sell that routine to." She smiled at him and turned to leave his office. Dr. Brainier fought hard to hold back a smile. She was the only nurse who could bring down his guard.

"Don't forget, Doctor, I'll be back later for that signature you promised me," Zurina said as the door closed behind her.

....

Iyon withdrew his blue rays from Jen's body. Dahlia entered the room with a small ceramic bowl containing a steamy potion.

THE WORLDS OF EARTH

"How far along is she with the medicine?"

"This is her second bowl, but I haven't noticed any change yet. Have you had any luck, Iyon?" Dahlia asked. She looked for a glimmer of hope in his eyes, but he kept them locked on Jen. Dahlia walked over and sat on a small wooden stool next to Jen's bedside.

"Jen is the same girl, but you have to help her realize this. You don't need me to tell you that Escapist has limited power."

"And apparently, so do I. My rays couldn't extend into her while I was there. Something else is preventing me from rescuing her, and I haven't been able to figure out what it is yet. I got so close to her, and was rubbing my head against her stomach, and I could not rescue her from that world. Escapist has something on her. Something I need to take care of."

Iyon stood in silence for a moment on the other side of Jen's bed.

"You'll find a way, Iyon. You always do."

Dahlia spoke with confidence. The remark made Iyon softly neigh. Through all the trials, tribulations, and loss that Dahlia had encountered during her life, she still managed to be optimistic.

"I need you to set up a cot here next to Jen's bed. I'm going to find someone else I can bring into that world with me."

"Of course, Iyon."

He left and headed for the temple. As Iyon landed with less than a graceful landing, the soldiers who were standing at attention immediately saluted him. Jared was among them. Iyon came to a halt and stood before them.

"At ease, men. My first mission to retrieve Jen failed. Now she's in a sanitarium that I can't enter, and is very likely the lair of Escapist herself. I need someone to get into that hospital and get her out of there, or alert me once she is found and I'll come charging."

Without hesitating, Jared stepped forward. "Sounds like old times. You know I wouldn't miss out on that fun."

Iyon nodded to his lifelong friend and fellow comrade. He knew Jared would be the one to volunteer without hesitation.

Then, changing the subject to another important matter, Iyon said,

73

"The newcomer, Jordan, is he resting comfortably?"

"Yes, but his news will mean nothing to us if we're unable to rescue Jen."

"Then let's go to Dahlia's. There's no time to lose."

Chapter 17
It's Showtime

Jared lay on a separate cot beside Jen. Iyon stood between them toward the end of the beds. With his eyes glowing, deep blue rays shot out to both Jen and Jared. The rays looked like gentle waves from the sea as it gently penetrated the both of them. Once in, it then bounced back to Iyon to connect with the gem on Iyon's collar, forming a mesmerizing double-sided V to some regard. As soon as all three of them were joined by the rays, Jared and Iyon were sent into the dream world where Jen was trapped.

....

Safely hidden in the woods, Jared and Iyon glared at the hospital. Jared was dressed in a black suit and a black and red striped tie with a slick black dress shirt to match. His dark brown hair was slicked back, transforming him into the persona he would need to get through the doors of the hospital.

"Well, good luck, 'Doctor.' I'll wait here for you. Find Jen quickly, Jared. If they begin any treatment on her, it may cause irreversible damage." As Jared turned to leave, Iyon added, "It might help you to know that Dr. Brainier wrote a book on schizophrenia and new modern cures. I saw a couple of the nurses reading it in the park the last time I was here. And don't forget the backup plan if this one fails."

Jared reached inside his suit jacket, feeling for his laser gun disguised as a pen. Iyon was able to superficially create one in that world. "Don't worry,

I haven't," he said reassuringly.

Jared turned to leave. "And signal me when you find her—I'll storm the walls once I know where she is," he called out.

"I got this, Iyon." With that, Jared left the woods and hurried up the street until he reached the entrance of the hospital. It was almost noon when Jared arrived at the locked doors. There was a small buzzer with a speaker on the wall to the right.

Jared pressed the buzzer and waited for a response.

"May I help you?" a pleasant voice said through the speaker.

"I hope so, ma'am. My name is Dr. David Shone. I happened to be in the area and I heard that Dr. Brainier is the chief of staff for this hospital. I recently studied his extraordinary book on schizophrenia, and I would greatly appreciate an opportunity to meet the man who wrote it."

"One moment, please." After a short pause the door beeped open, allowing Jared entrance through its impressive double frame. The first frame was made of wood. The second, however, was made of a metallic material. At first, Jared felt threatened, but no alarms sounded, so he kept going. Another security door opened. A young woman greeted Jared. She had deep brown eyes and long raven hair tied back in a ponytail. Her olive skin contrasted with her white nurse's uniform. She smiled, showing her pearly white teeth. Then she reached out her hand to shake his. She was strikingly beautiful. Jared struggled to maintain his professional composure.

"Dr. Shone, I presume. My name is Zurina, and I'll be taking you to see Dr. Brainier. Right this way, please."

Zurina opened another security door, and the two began walking down a long corridor.

"So, Zurina, how long have you been working with Dr. Brainier?" Jared asked in an effort to make light conversation with the attractive nurse who he had to enforce in his mind didn't actually exist.

Zurina smiled strangely when he said that. "I've been working here long enough, Dr. Shone." This wasn't the typical response that Jared had expected from what should have been a mindless hologram figure. His curiosity piqued, he decided to try to find out why Zurina seemed to dislike

Dr. Brainier.

"Too many demands perhaps?" he queried.

"Not exactly."

"Then what, exactly?"

"Let's just say I do whatever it is I need to do around here."

"If you're unhappy, then why bother staying?"

She smirked at that. "For the company of course, what else? I have my reasons and you have yours, Dr. Shone. Maybe we'll cross paths again before you leave today."

Definitely not a hologram, Jared concluded.

She stopped by a door with a keypad entry on the side, turned toward him and stared into his eyes. "Here you are, Doctor," she said as she opened the door for him. Then she hurried off without another word. Jared was captivated by Zurina's beauty, but there was more to her than that. He couldn't put his finger on it.

Jared entered the office and closed the door behind him, trying to get Zurina off his mind. Dr. Brainier looked up from his mahogany desk and stood to shake Jared's hand. He was a head shorter than Jared. His white doctor's coat hung down to his thighs, but it couldn't hide his plump belly. His grayish beard and mustache blended in with his pale complexion. A pair of black reading glasses sat on the end of his nose. Underneath this dowdy exterior was a brilliant man. Dr. Brainier had achieved great renown in the dream world by doing extensive research on the mind.

"Dr. Brainier, my name is Dr. David Shone, and I want to thank you for letting me intrude on you like this. It's a pleasure to meet the man behind the book that inspired me."

Dr. Brainier smiled broadly as he received this stranger's praise. "Well, thank you, young man," he said, beaming with pride. "Please have a seat. So, you also help the mentally ill."

Jared humbly smiled. "Yes, sir. Your book opened my eyes to new methods of curing schizophrenia."

The doctor sat and carefully sipped his steaming coffee. "Can I offer you a cup?"

"No, thank you."

Two quick knocks on the door was all the notice that was given and the office door suddenly opened. Zurina entered, not bothering to wait for permission. She walked over to the side of Dr. Brainier's desk, leaving him shocked and embarrassed.

"Zurina, what's the meaning of this?"

"I'm sorry to bother you, Doctor, but you promised to sign this form for me, and time is of the essence."

She leaned over the desk and slid the form that read HIGHLY CLASSIFIED in front of him. She batted her deep brown eyes at him while pointing at a line on the form.

"A quick signature is all I need, and then I'll leave so that you gentlemen can continue your conversation."

Mesmerized by her eyes, the doctor took the pen from inside his desk and signed his name on the form. Zurina mouthed a thank you at the doctor and sashayed out of the room, closing the door behind her.

Jared was stunned by the way Dr. Brainier was easily manipulated by Zurina.

"Interesting nurse you have there, Doctor."

"Ah, well, yes. I mean, I know she may not be the most professional nurse, but she's really good at her job."

I guess that's one way of putting it, thought Jared. He knew he needed to turn his attention back to Dr. Brainier before the doctor had a chance to notice that Jared's mind had drifted. However, the doctor was also preoccupied with thoughts of Zurina.

....

Zurina marched down the hallway on the lowest level of the hospital. She approached an entrance that had been forbidden to her until now. It had taken weeks of smiles, charming looks, and even a casual dinner to manipulate the doctor into giving her the highest clearance level.

At the end of the corridor was a foot-thick solid metal door. In front of it were two guards, armed with automatic weapons. Zurina made sure to display absolute confidence in front of them. She knew that any sign of nervousness would draw suspicion.

"Dr. Brainier sent me to get a couple of files. Here's the order sheet."

One of the guards snatched the clipboard from her, examined the form and studied her. Everything looked legitimate, so he opened the door to the confidential file room and let her in.

"You have five minutes," he said sternly.

As soon as the door shut behind her, Zurina got to work. Lining the walls were thousands of files, each containing a thin circular disk. Knowing that she didn't have much time, she ran first to the H section and found Jen's file. It read: Jennifer Hanning, extract pertinent information and terminate. Zurina removed the disk from that file and clasped it to the clipboard that she'd been carrying. She took the file of another patient who received routine treatment and hid Jen's disk in it.

Then, knowing that Jared was also in danger, she rushed to the J section where something immediately caught her eye. The name tag on one of the files in that section was glowing, signifying that the file had recently been activated. Zurina took a closer look. The file read:

Jared—

Rebel/Insurgent: apprehend and interrogate. WARNING: IDENTITY CONFIRMED. Entered the building at 12:05 p.m.

Jared had triggered the sensor when he entered the building, sending all of his information directly to his disk. It would only be minutes before Escapist would be notified and Jared captured. Realizing the danger was eminent, Zurina removed his file from the shelf and switched the magnetic name tag with that of another patient who was a long time prisoner. By the time she'd swapped the name tags, three minutes were already up.

Suddenly, a swirling vortex appeared in front of Zurina as she stood between the rows of files. A portal opened and out stepped a man dressed in soldier's uniform.

Zurina glared at him and whispered harshly, "What are you doing here? You'll blow my cover."

"Your mistress wants to know your status. She hates not being able to follow your movements," the soldier bluntly stated. "Is your plan going to work?"

"Yes, perfectly, but you must leave right away! I'll signal for pick up when I'm ready to go. It won't be long now."

"Very well, do you have any more strange requests for things you need?" he persisted.

"No. Please go."

He turned and disappeared through the portal in the vortex, which quickly vanished. Zurina ran to the exit and regained her composure just as the door slid open.

As was their custom, the guards detained Zurina, took the clipboard from her hand and examined the files that she had. The fear of possibly getting caught with Jen's disk and Jared's file was eating her up inside. One of the guards chuckled as he casually reviewed things. Zurina held her breath.

"I can't believe this old fool is still alive. Looks like you've got a busy day. Carry on," said the guard, handing the clipboard back to her.

Zurina laughed with him. "Thank you, I certainly will," she said, then quickly departed.

....

Dr. Brainier caught himself daydreaming about Zurina. He tried to cover it up, hoping Jared hadn't noticed.

"You know what?" he said. "I hardly ever do this, but if you want, I'll take you on a personal tour of the hospital and show you our new treatment center."

Jared stared at Dr. Brainier in disbelief. *Could it be this easy?* "Well, that would be wonderful....Only if you have time, Doctor. But it would be a great honor."

As Dr. Brainier stood up, a nurse came into the room. Sensing that the doctor was irritated by her interruption, she spoke fast. "You wished to be notified immediately, sir, when your new patient woke up."

"Ah, yes, thank you. Please have her taken to Waiting Room C. The work must start immediately with that one."

"Yes, right away, sir." She exited the room.

Dr. Brainier motioned Jared toward the door.

"Thanks for offering to take me on a tour of your facility," Jared said, "and will I be fortunate enough to see your work in action? Sounds like you have a hot case to work on," he concluded, smiling.

"Yes, it will be a great honor to work that case, but intense treatment will be used." Then looking quizzically at Jared, he continued, "In fact, she probably won't survive the night. So if you don't have the stomach for it, then you may not be able to watch." Dr. Brainier studied Jared's face intently, looking for any sense of compassion or deceitful response that would make him sound like a rebel. With all the hatred Jared had for what this doctor did to good people, he turned that hatred into the response he needed to produce. Shrugging his shoulders and throwing in a smirk as if he didn't have a care in the world, Jared looked squarely back at the doctor.

"I administer the treatments on my patients, Dr. Brainier. Why should the nurses have all the fun? I can manage, Doctor. I can manage just fine."

"Well, you sound pretty serious to me and I may just let you see it then, but you know, I've been so busy today that I haven't had a chance to eat. Let's have a quick snack first. Then I'll show you around."

Jared did his best to hide his disappointment by the delay. "Of course, Doctor," Jared said, knowing that every second lost endangered Jen's life.

Chapter 18
Rude Awakening

Jen stretched out, then curled up on her side. She thought that she was sleeping in her bed back at home, but the mattress felt stiff and unfamiliar. When she opened her eyes, she saw a dull tan wall instead of the vivid purple one she was used to. Jen was in a matchbox-sized room without any furniture except, of course, the bed. On the wall to her left near the ceiling was a small rectangular barred window. Jen's pulse raced as she took in her surroundings. As the sedative wore off, her mind cleared. She noticed she was wearing navy blue pajama bottoms and a large royal blue T-shirt—clothes that were not her own.

There was a clicking sound at the door as it was being unlocked. It opened and four stout nurses came in, rolling a gurney with straps all over it. Jen jumped off the bed and backed into a corner.

"Please. Stay away from me. I want to see my parents right now," Jen pleaded.

The nurses stared at her, emotionlessly.

"Jennifer Hanning, your parents have signed you over to the care of Dr. Brainier so you can get proper treatment. Now we can do this the easy way or the hard way. It's up to you," said the nurse whose nametag read Bertha.

Jen was quivering all over. She couldn't believe that her parents had put her in this place. "Wha…What is it you want me to do?" Jen asked fearfully.

"Lie down on this," another nurse, whose nametag said Mildred, who appeared to be the head nurse, commanded as she pointed with her clammy white finger to the gurney.

"If I don't give you any hassle, then that means no straps, right?"

"You're a patient here, Jennifer. You don't have the right to bargain with us. Straps are standard for all our patients during any transport. Last chance," Mildred said with a smirk.

Jen said nothing. All she could do was shake her head. There was no way she would voluntarily lie down. The four nurses moved into action, two flanked on each side of her. They grabbed her arms and legs. Picking her straight up, they carried her to the gurney, and slammed her down on it. Jen screamed, "No!" and tried to struggle, but within a minute, her hands, feet, and waist were strapped. Once tied down, Mildred injected her with a form of a sedative; just enough to take the fight out of her, but the potion used was also intended as punishment. The fluid burned as it was injected. Jen screamed in horror as the pain spread in her veins, so two straps were fastened over her head—one across her forehead and the other across her mouth so she couldn't scream anymore.

Mildred looked down at Jen and pinched her face where it wasn't covered with a strap. "You should've chosen the easy way, Jennifer, and then maybe I wouldn't have covered your mouth and given you that shot. The pain will wear off as you become drowsy. But every time you disobey us, you can count on getting that shot." Then, turning to the other nurses, she said, "Let's move out, ladies. Our orders are to take her to Waiting Room C. The treatment schedule is intense with this one and starts soon."

Jen was completely immobilized by her restraints and helpless to fight the pain of the injection as it spread across her body. All she could do was watch light after light on the ceiling and listen to the gurney's squeaky wheels as the nurses carted her down a hallway. Groans and cries rose from behind the locked doors. The stench of vomit drifted out of one room. Then a blood-curdling scream startled her. Jen's body tensed and she dug her fingers into the sides of the gurney. Finally, the sedative took effect, forcing her to relax her grip. Sounds became muffled, and she fought to stay awake.

When they reached the waiting room, the nurses input a code to gain entrance. The door slid open, and Jen was rolled into a bare round room. On the opposite side, another doorway led to the testing labs. In the center was a man strapped to a gurney.

"Hey, Bertha, why is Patient 63 still in here? He was supposed to start his second round of treatment two hours ago," Mildred said.

Bertha walked over to the man and checked to see if he was conscious. "Dr. Brainier ordered to wait an extra hour because this patient was convulsing so hard." She lifted his eyelid.

"He was completely unresponsive to the last treatment. So we'll have to leave Jennifer in here for a bit while a few more tests are administered on this one."

"I'm starving. Let's go have lunch first. The other nurses can handle Patient 63," Mildred said.

"Sounds good to me," Bertha said.

The nurses with Mildred nodded, then wheeled the old man out and handed him over to their colleagues. Then they carted Jen to his spot and locked the wheels in place.

Bertha leaned over Jen after the other nurses left and stared down into her scared blue eyes with the malicious look of one who thoroughly enjoys inflicting pain on others. Reaching between the straps, she grabbed one of Jen's cheeks and roughly pinched it. "I suggest you get some rest. You're gonna need it in order to survive the first round." She smiled wickedly, strolled away, and switched off the lights. As the door slid shut behind Bertha, Jen was left alone in the dark. She wanted so badly to fight the restraints, but her body was paralyzed. Soon, she could no longer fight and fell into a deep unconsciousness.

....

Every minute wasted in the lunchroom was painstakingly hard for Jared to endure. He wanted to find Jen and rescue her, yet he had to sit there and maintain his phony excitement while the doctor stuffed his face.

"I can't wait to see your facility. You don't know what it means to me," Jared said in an effort to hurry the doctor along.

Dr. Brainier finished the last bite of his steak and cheese sandwich. He wiped his mouth, speaking at the same time. "The honor is mine," he said with an obnoxious smile on his face.

While ostensibly looking for ways to treat a variety of mental illnesses, especially schizophrenia, Dr. Brainier was actually doing Escapist's bidding by seeking ways to unlock the secrets that people refused to reveal. That's what made it fun for him; when they finally cracked and secrets were revealed. They cried and whimpered and pleaded for death. Then, happily, he would let them die.

Doctor Brainier looked down at the sheet covering Jen's schedule, deciding whether or not to show this young doctor his newest addition.

Jared said, "You see, I'm treating a sixteen-year-old who's completely delusional, and I'm trying to decide what to do with her. She is seeing black I believe, among other things."

"Black, you say? Well, as you read in my book, I'm moving away from medication. I don't find it effective enough. You should transfer your patient to our facility where we have the necessary medical equipment and specially trained staff. Then I can show you the best way to treat that kind of condition."

"Sounds like a plan. I'd really appreciate an opportunity to observe your techniques."

Dr. Brainier stuck out his hand and the two shook on it.

"I will take you to the patient and give you direct access to see her."

They walked to an elevator at the end of the hallway. Dr. Brainier put his key in to access the elevator along with a retinal eye scan, and then the two entered. On their way to the lower level, Dr. Brainier warned Jared, "Don't forget I warned you about the intensity of this new work. It's all for the good of the cause."

The elevator doors opened and the two stepped into a corridor illuminated by a blue neon light. The buzz of electricity and an occasional male-sounding shriek echoed in the distance. Wires and tubes of all sizes lined the walls. Dr. Brainier and Jared proceeded until they reached a ceiling-mounted metal door at the end of the hallway. After Dr. Brainier entered a code on the key pad, the door opened and the two men walked into an observatory. As they approached a glass wall, Jared and Dr. Brainier peered through the window and saw, strapped down on a table, a poor fellow with dozens of wires attaching him to a monstrosity of a machine.

"You see that patient down there? After being interrogated, he finally confessed that our beautiful world had turned black and that the wind was calling his name. Our job is to probe his subconscious mind to see what he is hiding from us. When we find cases like this, we know we are dealing with spies. So their rights are written off and we are free to use whatever is necessary to retrieve the information."

A sick feeling overwhelmed Jared as he stared down at the dying man and saw just how horrific and torturous the interrogations were that took place here. It was obvious to Jared now that Escapist knew that there were spies in her world, and she would go to any length to find them. He had to get to Jen, get out, and deliver all this information to Iyon.

Dr. Brainier noticed the worried look on Jared's face.

"We use these patients to do research for Dr. E. She demands to know where their visions stem from. Then we reprogram them to work for her if at all possible."

Realizing that he had failed to hide his consternation, Jared regained his composure and asked, "So is this currently your only patient in this condition? It doesn't look like I'll get to see much action from this guy."

"No. My next one will be coming in the room in a few minutes. The next one in is a teenage girl."

"Am I allowed to talk to her before she goes in? I'd like a chance to record what she says," Jared said excitedly.

"Yes, the door to the lab is straight through there and you are free to go." Dr. Brainier pointed to a door in the corner and Jared proceeded to it. As he reached for the knob, the sound of a metal door slamming was heard. Jared spun around and saw that Dr. Brainier was gone.

"Dr. Brainier, please report to Mainstay," a woman's chilling voice said over the central intercom.

Along with that door, another more impenetrable-looking security door came down in front of it. Jared ran to the windows but bars slid down, securely locking him in the room. Jared looked over to the corner and saw a camera following his every move and all vents in the room sealed shut. His cover had obviously been blown, so in retaliation he pulled out the pen and destroyed the camera. Jared's mind raced. He knew he was close to Jen's location and didn't want to wait for the doctor to return with reinforcements. He had to figure out how to escape and get to Jen fast. He pressed on his beacon to alert Iyon but there was no signal at all. He ran back to the door in the corner and grabbed the knob, but he had been tricked. It was nothing but part of the wall. He shot at the window with his laser weapon, thinking it would be the easiest to destroy, but the laser bounced off and bounced from wall to wall wildly. Jared hit the ground until the laser finally collided with a chair and eradicated it. The very faint sound of gas entering the room was the next sound he heard.

Chapter 19
Saving Jen

Dr. Brainier sheepishly crept into a vaulted room to meet with the one known as Escapist. She sat in a black leather chair that creaked as she turned to face him. Her skin was freakishly pale, and her black dress made her appear like death itself. With her sapphire eyes, she stared down at the wretched man.

"This Dr. Shone, do you know anything about him?" she asked brusquely.

Dr. Brainier fidgeted nervously. Her presence always had that effect on him.

"Well, ma'am, he's a doctor who treats schizophrenics and has a patient with similar symptoms to those of Jennifer Hanning. He also said he'd be willing to bring the patient here for us to work on. But his story seemed too good to be true so he has been secured until I can verify his credentials."

"His credentials have been verified and he is one of our most wanted. He is highly dangerous. His real name is Jared and we have been searching for others that could be with him. So far nothing has come up."

She paused for a short moment, then continued, "Well, I assume you created a file and disk for this rebel the second he entered the building."

"Yes, ma'am, that's our usual procedure," said Dr. Brainier, as beads of perspiration formed on his forehead.

"I assume you want me to interrogate him?"

Escapist sighed disgustedly and said, "Yes, that's exactly what I want. But make sure this one doesn't die. A message will be sent to higher command that we have him detained. Break him piece by piece if you have to. Now go!"

With that, two Amazon-looking women in dark suits grabbed Dr. Brainier and shoved him out of the room. As soon as the door was shut behind him, the doctor called security and ordered a band of armed men to meet him in the corridor near the observatory. Dr. Brainier stormed into the storage room and seized a large stun gun. Finally, a chance to administer all his methods of interrogation with no holds barred. Dr. Brainier's eyes went bloodshot as hunger and rage festered inside him with an intense desire to create great pain for his victim.

The security team surrounded the entrance of the room detaining Jared, readied their weapons, and waited for Dr. Brainier's command.

"All right, men, let's make this quick. He's trapped. Set your guns to stun because we need him alive," Dr. Brainier ordered.

With that, the chief officer pressed in the code, and the group charged into the observatory.

....

As soon as Jared heard the sound of the gas, he took in the largest breath of clean air possible. Combat had trained him to hold his breath for several minutes, but then what?

Down below, they wheeled a patient out and prepared the machine for the next victim, which he knew was Jen. The nurse from below looked up at Jared and laughed. It gave Jared the sick feeling that they were going to make him watch them torture Jen.

When Jared was down to his last minute of breath, the sound of air came from behind him, as well as something opening. Jared dropped to his knees, spun around, and looked, with weapon in hand. There toward the ground, part of the wall opened, revealing a small tunnel. As it opened, Zurina's head popped out with a mask over her mouth and nose. She quickly tossed one to Jared and signaled him into the tunnel. He threw the mask over his face and crawled into the tunnel.

"Help me close it, fast!" she yelled through her mask.

Jared grabbed the lever and the door sealed shut, locked from the inside with several metal levers.

"I knew he would do this. It's how he always catches you guys. He fills the room with gas that causes paralysis but you remain conscious. Then he straps you to a table and positions it vertical. He would have forced you to watch Jen be tortured. Come on, Jared. I know where Jen is but we have to move fast! And keep the mask on until we get to the next vent shaft so the gas doesn't paralyze you."

Jared couldn't believe she knew his real name and that she seemed to be there to help him. Not sure if he could trust her yet, he hesitantly put his weapon back in his suit jacket and said, "All right, but who are you?"

"I don't have time to explain. Obviously, Escapist is on to you. If she catches you, you'll be tortured until she gets what she wants. We're in front of the enemy by only a couple of minutes."

Jared was surprised by how much the woman knew, and the fact that she knew his identity played with his ego horribly. Zurina started crawling through the vent ahead of him. "Fine, just stay in front of me."

Zurina responded with an order of her own. "No more talking until I say or they'll hear us. And like I have any other options here, Jared. Of course I'm in front—I'm leading the way."

"Does the doctor know about the tunnel?" he whispered.

"No! No one knows cuz I spent weeks cutting through the steel on my breaks to make the opening. Now, come on!"

As fast as they could, the two crawled in silence through the passageway that led them close to Jen's room.

Chapter 20
The Chase Continues!

As soon as the green light came on indicating the room was free of gas, the officers stormed the observatory with their guns blasting, expecting to find an easy target lying helpless on the ground. All they hit were walls. Dr. Brainier charged in after them, eager to inflict pain. He grew livid as he looked across the empty room.

Taking hold of Digon, the officer who was standing next to him, he shouted, "You find me that man!"

Dr. Brainier shook Digon, then let him go. He and the others hurried down the corridor. Meanwhile, the doctor called his head nurse.

Mildred was just sitting down for lunch when her phone rang. She set her sandwich aside and calmly answered, "Mildred here."

"Mildred, I want Jen carted to the treatment room and worked on now. I want to be reading her mind by the end of the hour. Be quick about it; we have a code red situation."

Completely numb to the suffering she'd inflicted on people, Mildred nonchalantly responded, "Sir, you know that will probably kill her."

"I don't care. All that matters is what we get out of her. I want it started at once."

"Yes, sir."

Mildred hung up her phone and spoke to the nurses looking at her expectantly from across the table. "Well, ladies, it looks like we've got work to do." They took one last bite of their sandwiches, and left the cafeteria in a rush.

Meanwhile, Dr. Brainier barked more orders over his phone at Digon. "Seal all the exits. Lock up every patient. Search each corridor room by room. Get a squad of men to Waiting Room C! And confound it, sound the alarm and flash the lights!"

....

Zurina and Jared reached the ventilation system. Jared followed Zurina through the thick darkness until they came to an opening. Zurina pushed the vent open, slid into the room, and groped her way to the light switch. She adjusted the light to dim. There in the center was Jen, strapped tightly to a gurney.

Jared slid out of the vent and dashed to the entrance. He pulled out his laser gun and blasted the keypad, vaporizing it instantly.

"Get the back door, too," Zurina whispered.

Jen made no response. The sedative had her knocked out.

"I was afraid of this. Let me give her a quick shot to wake her up," Zurina said.

Once she did that, Jared and Zurina made quick work of ripping her straps off. Jen's eyes started to open. Zurina spoke softly to her, "Jen, my name is Zurina, and this is Jared. Your life is in terrible danger, but you are safe with us. Don't be afraid, just come with us, okay hon?"

Jen didn't recognize either of them, but she nodded her head in affirmation. If it meant getting out of that room, then she would trust them. The alarms started going off in the building. Zurina looked nervously at Jared. "They'll be here any minute. We'll have to take her back through the vent and up to the roof. But then we'll be trapped, unless Iyon is with you. Please tell me he is?"

"Yes," Jared bluntly responded. "I don't know how you know about us, but when this is over, you will need to do some explaining."

With Jen in his arms, Jared and Zurina ran to the vent. Zurina climbed in first.

"Do you think you can crawl through the vent, Jen?" Jared asked.

Jen nodded weakly, but her body was shaking. He lifted her up to the vent, then went in last, replacing the grate behind him. The sounds of the guards came from the other side of the door.

The three carefully wended their way upwards through the ventilation system; several times they had to help Jen as the feebleness slowly wore off. Finally, they reached a vertical shaft that led up to the roof. From the top of the shaft hung a rope with knots tied in it that Zurina had prepared for this very reason. After she began climbing, Jen was to go next. Jen reached for the rope and tried to climb, but her foot slipped and she fell clumsily on top of Jared, who did his best to catch her. He could hear a commotion in the vents behind them. Dr. Brainier's men were moving through them fast.

"Quick! Get on my back and hold on tight!"

Jen did her best to comply. Jared grabbed the rope and climbed as fast as he could, for he knew their lives depended on his speed. As soon as Zurina reached the roof, she spun around and helped Jen up. The minute Jen stepped onto the roof, she tripped, fell and hit her head on the ventilation shaft and went unconscious. Zurina gasped in disbelief. She bent down, grabbed Jen and propped her up against the side of the vent shaft. Jared crawled onto the roof, pulled out his weapon and blasted the rope, disintegrating it. He pressed down on his watch, sending a sound frequency to summon Iyon then looked at Zurina whose eyes were quivering by now.

"Jared, this is bad. We have to wake her up!"

Jared's frustration peaked and he snapped, "Iyon will take care of it. Who you are and how do you know about us?"

"I was sent here from another world to help those that are imprisoned by Escapist. My life is complicated and hard to explain, but our sources told us that Jen would more than likely end up here because the enemy wants her any way they can get her."

Hearing the guards approaching the bottom of the vent, Zurina and Jared kept quiet on the rooftop until the soldiers moved on.

"How do you know about me?" he demanded.

"Am I interrupting something?" asked Iyon, who'd come out of the woods and flown to the roof to find them.

"Not at all," Zurina replied. "I was trying to explain to your comrade who I am. But surely you don't forget a face, or a pair of eyes, do you?"

Iyon stared into the young woman's eyes for a second before he was interrupted by the sounds of guards.

"There they are!" shouted Digon, who'd climbed the stairs to the roof and was no more than twenty yards away. He raised his laser to shoot but was vaporized by Jared's weapon.

Zurina pulled the small, thin disks from her jacket pocket and threw them on the ground in front of Jared.

"Destroy these, Jared. Otherwise, you and Jen will both be trapped here."

He stared warily at the disks and refused. "How do I know what plans you might have for Jen?"

The guards now poured onto the ceiling from all over and began shooting at them.

"Jared, now!" she commanded, but instead he started firing at the guards.

Iyon stared at the disks and blasted them into fine particles. Jared glanced at Iyon with a questioning look but returned to firing at the enemy, knowing better not to question Iyon's decision.

Iyon's eyes glared dark blue, and eradicated one whole squad of guards from the rooftop and it was then that he felt her presence. Escapist was coming. The encounter would be unavoidable.

....

While Jared and the others were making their way to the roof, Escapist was anxiously pacing back and forth in her lair. A dark dimensional window appeared on the wall and her skin mutated into red scales as her body expanded. Horns grew out of her head and her face transformed. The clothes she was wearing shredded and fell to the floor. Escapist had changed herself back into her original form of a red dragon. Her paws pounded the ground. Looking at the dark dimensional window, she saw a black hole emerge from within a whirling storm. Within that black hole appeared a dark gray cloud that formed the face of another dragon. It was Dolorous. Escapist bowed to the ground out of respect for her superior.

"General, to what do I owe the honor of...."

"Silence!" Dolorous fumed. "You were sent here to control this world and search out our enemies. But what do I find instead?"

Escapist stuttered, unable to respond.

"I see your world is out of control. I see that you, Escapist, have failed to obtain the information we need. You have dealt weakly with these humans, and now the girl that we suspect to be the Key Holder is trying to escape to the roof with one of our mortal enemies, Iyon!"

Escapist growled Iyon's name under her breath. Dolorous roared and snarled from within the dimensional window. If he could've entered her world, he would've torn Escapist to pieces.

"These are your orders, Escapist," he said furiously. "Get that girl back from Iyon. He thinks he can just whisk her away like the others, but I know you still have her mind trapped here. When he realizes his efforts are futile, he will have no choice but to leave her behind. Get the information we need and destroy her!"

"Yes, General, as you wish," she said humbly.

"Fail our Master again, and you'll be taken to his personal dungeon," Dolorous warned.

Escapist didn't speak, but continued to bow until Dolorous was gone and the dimensional window faded away. Then she got up and snarled at her servants, "Go to the file room and bring me Jennifer's and Jared's disks."

The two women bowed to the ground and replied, "Mistress, your faithful servant, Goba, has already gone to retrieve them. She should be here any moment."

A few seconds later, Goba came trembling through the door and fell down before Escapist.

"Mistress, please forgive us all, but the disk for the girl is gone. It was picked up this morning by a nurse. And the file for the one you believe to be Jared is missing also. It was somehow swapped out with the file of an older patient. Please don't be angry with me, Mistress. I'm just the messenger!" Goba cried as she bowed low before the dragon.

Escapist became so enraged by this news that fire exploded from her mouth, instantly eradicating Goba. Escapist blew the doors apart as she roared and galloped out of the room. Her only chance of survival would be to destroy Iyon herself before he could escape with Jen.

....

"Iyon!" Zurina yelled. "Jen is still unconscious! You can't take her from here until she comes to, or she'll never wake up in the real world."

"Fire at will!" shouted one of the guards. Blasts hit all around the vent shaft where Zurina hid with Jen. Iyon rose on his hind legs, his mane and metallic tail whipping wildly. He emitted another giant blue laser from his eyes and it swept across the rooftop, taking out the entire front squad that had surrounded them. From the other side of the building, the roof blew apart and out flew Escapist.

Iyon snorted and said, "Jared, wake her up now!"

"Give me that girl, Iyon," hissed the beast as she advanced toward him.

Iyon reared back on his hind legs and then pounded the ground fiercely.

Jared and Zurina shook Jen by the shoulders, trying to wake her. Bullets whizzed all around them, so they remained pressed against the vent shaft to avoid being shot.

Escapist roared and charged Iyon. He charged right back. The two collided with fire and lasers blazing at one another. Iyon's metallic tail wrapped around Escapist's horns as she gashed him several times, digging her claws as far into him as she could, hoping to reach the heart. Bolts of electricity ignited her body. Iyon pulled his tail that was wrapped around her horns, spun her around and threw her off the roof. That gave him the time he needed.

Iyon ran to Jen. Taking one strand of his tail, he pressed it into her chest. "I'm sorry for this pain, Jen," Iyon said and zapped her body with the least amount of electrifying power that he could send out.

Jen's eyes popped open and she gasped for breath. She looked up at Zurina and cried, "Get me out of here!"

Escapist regained control and flew back to the roof. Upon landing, she inhaled deeply and blew out a powerful force of fire and energy. Iyon was bleeding profusely, but put his pain out of his mind. He turned toward the approaching blaze and counter-attacked with his own incredible display of power filled with blue lightning and energy that sent Escapist spinning backwards.

Jared fell to Jen's side and held her tightly.

"Give me your weapon, Jared. I'll cover you while you and Jen make your escape," Zurina said. Jared handed her the weapon. Zurina took a quick step away and continued firing at the guards.

"Iyon, now!" Jared yelled.

With guns blasting all around them, and even hitting Iyon at times, he formed a metallic force field that surrounded Jen and Jared. Within a few seconds, the three of them were gone.

Zurina was left on the roof to face the enemy alone. She signaled for the portal from her own secret device hidden in her pocket, and then continued firing at the enemy, showing no mercy. At that moment, Dr. Brainier arrived on the roof. He looked and saw the woman who was responsible for destroying his life and now his heart. The doctor stood, stunned and speechless. He dropped his weapon and stared one last time at her. A vortex appeared next to Zurina. She didn't bother to give Dr. Brainier one last look as she dropped Jared's gun and jumped into the portal, vanishing from the dream realm.

When Escapist saw that she had been defeated, she roared miserably, letting out a violent blast that blew across the entire roof, engulfing everyone on it, including Dr. Brainier. Suddenly, a strong wind threw her off the roof. Escapist was pinned to the ground by a much greater power. A huge vortex opened up in the sky and a monstrous dragon emerged, crying chains in its mouth. The Dungeon Master had come for her. Escapist's paws were chained together. Her echoing screams faded as she was dragged through the air and into the enormous swirling mass that led to the realm of pain and punishment where she would be mercilessly tortured for her failure.

Chapter 21
A Risky Game, Indeed

John knew he didn't have much time before the Skeign found him again. He searched the abandoned safe house for the bag of fruit that Jen and the others had left behind. He found it beside the cot, grabbed it and quickly disappeared. He knew as long as he kept rotating positions every couple of minutes, Felonious wouldn't be able to catch him.

After many hours of this cat and mouse chase, John became exhausted and wished he could allow himself to fall asleep because then he would be untraceable. But he also knew it was unwise to do until he was in a safe house. So, John pictured one and instantly found himself in a small cave. The entrance had been sealed off, leaving him at first in utter darkness. However, the ring that Hope had given him triggered a lantern on a small limestone table, providing him with enough light to see. John wearily walked toward the lantern and sat down on the moist dirt ground. He opened the bag of fruit, yanked one out and devoured it.

Feeling more relaxed, he lay down on his back and thought of his remarkable daughter and how brave she'd become. If only he could be with her. The hardest thing he ever had to do was push her away. But at least she was with Iyon, and the key was safe in their possession. His thoughts lingered on his daughter until he drifted off to sleep. John was safe, for the moment.

....

The blue rays that joined Iyon, Jen and Jared at Dahlia's home dissipated. Iyon nudged the other two with his nose, making sure they were okay. Jared opened his eyes and looked over at Jen, who was waking up. Dahlia was also there, sitting on the stool next to Jen's bedside.

"Welcome back, Jen," Dahlia said, her tone delicate and gentle.

Jen looked up and saw two people and a white horse standing over her. Iyon was completely drenched in sweat but not bleeding. She didn't know who they were, where she was, or how she had gotten there. She couldn't even remember her own self for that matter.

"What do we do? She doesn't remember us," Jared said.

"Jen," Iyon spoke, which made Jen stare at Iyon, wide-eyed.

"She needs something from her home to help trigger her memory." Dahlia got up and walked over to the closet and took out the backpack she had come with. She walked to Jen's bedside and gave it to her.

"Here, Jen, do you remember this?"

Jen looked at the leather backpack and flashes of her father having it with him everywhere he went, filled her mind. Tears streamed down her face as the memories poured into her. The wonderful runs they had together, and the dinners as a family; then ushered in her father's disappearance, the pain of all the rejection from friends and even family. And then ushered in the memories of the present day when she very last saw her father. Ignited by that thought, she popped straight up and looked at Iyon, "The key! He gave me a key. Where is it?"

Dahlia put her hand on Jen's shoulder. "It's okay. We have the key. Don't push yourself too fast, Jen. You've been on death's doorway for a couple days now."

Still feeling feeble, Jen relaxed. She turned and looked at Iyon and Jared, gratitude in her eyes.

"I remember everything you did for me when I was trapped. Thank you for coming for me." Jen sat up, put her head next to Iyon's forehead, and stroked the side of his neck.

It wasn't Iyon's custom to let too many show him affection, or to let himself become attached, but this one was creeping quickly into the deep parts of his heart, and for the first time, this Warrior was unable to stop it.

For a moment, the room was silent, and then a rumbling in Jen's stomach broke the peaceful stillness.

"I'm starving."

Dahlia smiled at Jen. "Well, you're in the right place for that."

Iyon said, "I have a few matters to attend to. Rest and recuperate. I'll return for you shortly."

"Okay, but let me know about my mom and dad as soon as you can.'

"I will as soon as I find out."

Iyon trotted out of the house, but stopped by the road leading to the village to wait for Jared.

Jared looked at Jen and smiled tenderly. "I'm glad you're back."

"It's good to be back. Thanks for helping to get me back," Jen spoke sincerely to him.

Jared left Dahlia's and hurried to meet Iyon on the road.

Chapter 22
On the Road to the Village

The well-trodden road was scattered with pebbles and stones. Jared was unusually quiet and kicked rocks as he walked by Iyon's side. Sensing that something was bothering his friend, Iyon asked, "What's on your mind, Jared?"

"It's Zurina. She knew so much about us, and I knew nothing about her. She acted as if you knew her. Is that true?"

"I don't actually know her, but I recognize her. She's one of our own, Jared, a citizen of Tranquil Earth, and I've seen her before, staring into my eyes from her hiding place. It was the day Tran was attacked, and I was busy rescuing all those I could. I wanted to go and get her, but the Skeign were right behind me. Later when I went back, I couldn't find her. Until now, I thought she was dead."

When Iyon paused for a moment, Jared interjected, "I hope you don't blame yourself, Iyon. Her current circumstance isn't your fault. At least now you know that she's alive, and it appears that she can handle herself quite brilliantly. Do you have any idea where she could be?"

"No, I don't. And how she came to be in the world of Escapist is yet another mystery. I'll talk to Hope and see what she has to say."

The two reached a fork in the road and stopped.

"Jared, I want you to go to the house where Jordan is being cared for. Check up on him. I'll go to Hope. Jen asked about the whereabouts of her mother, and I don't know if Hope has had any success in finding her."

"Okay, Iyon. I'll report back when I'm finished."

After that, Iyon and Jared separated, each going his own way.

Chapter 23
Onward

For the next two days, Jen sat down to the most terrific meals, next to her mother's, that she'd ever eaten. She spent time resting and talking to Dahlia about the way of life in Tolare. Dahlia took Jen in as if she were her own and had a special tunic made for her out of Tolare's finest material. She braided Jen's hair and pinned it up. Refreshed and full of life, Jen was talking and laughing with Dahlia in her garden when Iyon came looking for her.

Iyon approached the backyard and delicately made his way along the path through Dahlia's exotic plants, careful to avoid crushing so much as a single flower or vegetable with his giant hooves. It wasn't until he reached the center of the garden that he found the two.

Jen was sitting on an intricately carved wooden bench with Dahlia. She was in the middle of laughing and then she turned and saw him. "Iyon!" She jumped up, ran to the great stallion and put her arms around his neck. "I was beginning to wonder when you'd come and check on me. Do you have any news?"

Iyon hesitated. He had looked into the eyes of so many people who were haunted by memories of their villages burned and their loved ones taken away: mothers without children, children without parents, fathers who'd lost their families. Now after spending time with Dahlia, Jen's eyes glistened with renewed hope, so it pained Iyon to have to give her bad news. Jen would have to be told that her father was still trapped in Shadow Earth and that her mother was nowhere to be found. Iyon wrapped his head around Jen's back and gently squeezed her. "You'll be answered today, Jen. But first, there are a few things I need to show you. Come, climb on my back."

Jen asked no more questions. She took hold of the collar and climbed on. Iyon slowly backed out of the garden. He looked up at Dahlia, who was watching them leave. She was smiling faintly, yet the hint of sadness in her eyes was evident.

"Thank you again, Dahlia, for taking care of Jen."

"I'll see you soon, Dahlia, and thank you for everything," said Jen.

Dahlia nodded and went back to work, tending to her garden.

....

When John woke, he found himself sitting alone in a cave with his knees bent in toward his chest. As he rested his hands on his knees, John lowered his head and began to sob. The realization of the destruction of the one way home was setting in. How would he ever see his family again? He tried to pull himself together.

I'm not giving up, he thought as he continuously pictured his daughter with the key. *She'll find a way back to me, I know she will.*

Then John started reminiscing about walking in the woods with his wife, falling into the light, and seeing Jen's smiling face in the cave where she found him. All of a sudden, Jen's face faded away. He tried to bring back her image, but he couldn't. Sensing danger, he tried to send himself into a continuous travel state. But something was wrong. John couldn't picture any of the safe houses, or any caverns, or any places he normally could travel to.

Then, he felt it. John's legs, arms, waist, and even his head were wrapped in tentacles, squeezing him until he cried out in pain. Felonious' Skeign had found him. The dark power that surged through their tails deadened all of John's thoughts. He was barely conscious, unable to move or think.

Felonious triumphantly approached his long-awaited prisoner and breathed his ghastly breath into John's nostrils. The smell was so horrible it caused John to gag. Felonious smiled, exposing his shark-like teeth. Then, looking at John's hand and realizing that the key wasn't there, Felonious bellowed, "Where is the key, human? Where did you hide it?"

John could barely breathe by now but he forced out, "You'll never find it."

"We'll see about that. With the poison in you now, your traveling days are over. You won't remain silent for long. You will tell me where the key is. And then you will be handed over to the Master."

Felonious gave an order to the Skeign holding John, "Take him to the dungeon! And keep him intoxicated."

John was carried through their portal that took them straight to the ghastly entrance to the dungeons of Shadow Earth. The horde roared with glee. They swung John around like a puppet, moving his hands and feet in whatever direction they pleased. They hissed and snarled in his face and watched his body shake at the stench of their poison-filled breath which also kept him intoxicated.

Those gruesome creatures then took John down into the depths where pure evil thrived.

Chapter 24
The Key Holder

Iyon broke into a gallop as he approached the spot where Jen had collapsed when she'd been enslaved in the dream world. As the temple came into view, so did the many soldiers who were standing guard. When Iyon reached them, he slowed to a walk. They stepped aside, allowing him access to the temple's center. Jen was so impressed by the incredible display of soldiers that she didn't notice when Iyon came to a halt. He lowered his head to the ground and gently neighed in order to get Jen's attention. She shifted her focus from the soldiers to where Iyon wanted her to look, and then she saw it. There in the middle of the circle lay the key that had fallen from her hand several days ago.

Curious as to why it was still lying there, Jen slid off Iyon's back and bent down to pick it up. All the guards and even Iyon held their breath as she grasped the key. This was the moment they'd dreamed of for such a long time. Holding the key tightly, she stood up and looked at Iyon. A quick sound of thanks and praise was heard across the crowd, leaving Jen perplexed at their excitement over such a small thing.

"Has the key been lying here all this time?" Jen asked in confusion.

Iyon stepped forward and entered the circle. "No one in this world has the ability to pick it up."

"I don't understand. Why not?"

"Hold out the key as if you were giving it to someone." Jen held it out and the guards closest to her approached to take the key. But each time they tried to grasp it, their hands passed right through as if it weren't there. Then Iyon approached and tried to take the key in his mouth, but it was as if he were nipping at air.

Feeling both perplexed and afraid, Jen said, "Okay, now I'm really confused. Why am I the only one who can pick up this key, and what does it open?"

"In time you'll discover why. For now, Hope has been waiting to see you."

Jen stared at the key for a moment and put the chain holding the key around her neck. After tucking it into her tunic, she climbed on Iyon's back. He struck the center with his hoof and the circular floor turned clockwise, lowering the two of them to the chamber where Hope resided. The opening above them closed fast, and the platform floated downward through the darkness. This time, Jen knew what to expect.

In front of her was the massive tree with its roots floating beneath it. The radiant light that beamed from within it filled the room and increased Jen's strength.

"Jen," called Hope, "It's good to see that you are fully recovered. Thanks to you and your father, the key has been found and brought back to us after so many years. Now we are one step closer to victory.

"A number of years ago, a strange presence came into the land. Though we felt it, we couldn't discern who or what it was, until it was too late. We eventually discovered that it was a man from True Earth who had found his way into our world. The man's name was Nyx. He cleverly won the hearts of many with his meekness and smooth talk. He befriended all the guards and people in high places and became well-connected. Once he did this, he subtly manipulated the officials into sharing the secrets of our land. Since the people of Tranquil Earth lived in peace and harmony, those in charge were entirely too trusting. They unwisely told Nyx about our secret treasure tucked away in a guarded vault in the inner temple. They gave away information about the mysterious key.

"So one day, Nyx talked one of his influential friends into

accompanying him to the inner temple so he could see the treasure. As soon as he beheld the key, he killed his friend and the guard. After locking their bodies in the vault, he slipped out of the temple, unnoticed.

"No one ever saw him again, nor was there any trace of the key. It's still a mystery how he was able to pick up and abscond with the key since only a pure-hearted Key Holder is supposed to be able to handle it. Nyx evidently had the power to prevent the Warrior Horses and even the key itself from detecting his inner evil. This is a dark chapter in the history of Tranquil Earth.

"We ourselves had no idea where the key could have been hidden all these years. But when your father came, something compelled him to explore Shadow Earth. I believe the key was summoning him, wanting to be found. Somehow your father evaded the Skeign and secured the key for us. Jen, to the people of this world, your father is a hero."

Hope stopped speaking. Jen sat spellbound, trying to take in everything her dad had become. Jen realized her life would never again be the same. She would have to accept the fact that she and her father had become engulfed in a war that she could barely comprehend. So in response, she said the only thing she could think of, "Hope, did you find my dad?"

"Not yet."

Jen choked up. She paused for a moment and pressed the key hidden under her clothes against her chest. With her heart beating strongly against the key, Jen whispered a quiet vow. "You risked everything to get this and sacrificed yourself to keep it safe. I won't let you down, Dad, I won't let you down." She lowered her hand and continued with her questions.

"And what about my mom?"

Hope didn't respond right away.

"You promised you would stop at nothing to find her. Is she okay?"

"What I have to tell you isn't easy."

Jen's heart pounded.

"Your mother is no longer on True Earth."

Jen was momentarily relieved. "Then you found her, right?"

"No, I cannot find her anywhere, not even in her dreams. I know this situation seems dire, but we'll find a way of getting them both back. I should warn you that it's going to require a great deal from you."

Jen got a lump in her throat upon hearing this news. Gazing into Hope's glow, Jen said, "Whatever it takes."

"Very well. According to the book of the Ancient Truths, there lies in one of these dimensional worlds of Earth an artifact, as old as time itself, known as the River Chest. Those who open the chest will find a mighty river of light flowing with untold power.

"The Ancient Truths went on to say that only a Key Holder has the power to physically handle and unlock the chest. But, once unlocked, anyone who is there can access the power inside. If you are evil, then that beauty which is inside will be forever tainted. Jordan, the new refugee from Pure Earth, told us a story that he heard from a couple of the elders of his world about a mysterious wooden chest engraved with gold and deemed untouchable. He said the elder lived in the city of Eshron, so that is where we will start. I believe that is the chest we seek.

"Jen, you are a Key Holder. You must go to Pure Earth and find the River Chest. We will be willing to compensate the people who dwell there for it, no matter the cost. With the power of the chest on our side, we will have a chance at winning this dark war, but it will also give you the ability to retrieve both of your parents. This time Iyon will be going with you," Hope said. Then she asked Iyon, "Will you want others to go with you?"

"No, I don't think it would be wise. A smaller party will be less conspicuous. If you feel you must, then send them quietly after Jen and I have arrived."

Hope's glow changed to deep yellow as Iyon prepared to travel through with Jen on his back.

"Are you ready for this, Jen?" Iyon asked.

She nodded. "As ready as I'll ever be."

Iyon stepped forward and the two were drawn into the portal. In a few seconds, they were standing on a beach.

Chapter 25
The People of Eshron
and Their Queen

Jen gazed across the glimmering ocean. The ivory sun reflected off the silvery waters. The waves rhythmically lapped the sandy shoreline. Iyon started with a trot and then shot to a full gallop as he headed toward a tall wall of dagger-like cliffs.

Within the rugged cliffs and mountain systems of this world lay a well-fortified city that had remained untouched from outsiders for a number of centuries. Very few knew of its existence, and its new leader wanted it kept that way. At the edge of the city was a small grassy field, and beyond that, an ancient castle stood proudly near the foot of a mountain. To the south of the castle was a forest, whose trees towered hundreds of feet into the air.

Beneath the castle and the entire city were a number of caves and hidden tunnels. One of those tunnels led to a mystical swirling vortex whose existence had been hidden for many years. Celesta, the queen of Eshron, had discovered this rare and unusual vortex some time ago. It was a portal that possessed the power of letting others travel through it. It also enabled them to see their world and others' as well.

Sidian, the general of the Eshron army, assigned a soldier daily to peer through the vortex to search for anyone infiltrating their domain. Regardless of whether an intruder was good or bad, the queen had recently decided that the visitor would never be allowed to leave their land again. If a foreigner were released, then Celesta felt that individual could jeopardize her in some way.

As a young soldier was looking through the portal, he spotted a horse and rider charging toward the cliffs. Without hesitation, he sounded the alarm. Within seconds, the general was notified and readied his troops for an assault. A group of twenty men geared with ropes, nets, guns, and lasers assembled in front of the portal as the proud cadet showed them his discovery. Sidian commanded the portal to reveal a nearby cave where his men could hide out and take the visitors by surprise. The troops rushed through and were soon stationed in the cave.

Sidian stayed behind. As he watched the attack from the control room, he heard soft footsteps coming down the rocky stairs. Recognizing those footsteps, he immediately stood at attention. Normally, a general would take great pride in serving his king or queen, but this was not the case with Sidian. Over the years, he noticed that the queen's greed and interest in black magic were consuming her. The soldiers and servants inside the castle also knew her sorcery was transforming her, but they would not dare mention it because going against the queen would result in torture or even death.

The people of Eshron had no idea how treacherous their queen had become. They trusted her implicitly and did all they could to please her.

Sidian was greatly saddened by this whole situation, yet he felt powerless to do anything about it. So he remained silent, feeling more like a subservient soldier than an officer. He obeyed every command, no matter how preposterous, given by his queen, but it was shameful to him.

When he heard the footsteps stop right behind him, Sidian turned around and bowed his head. "My Queen," he humbly and respectfully said. "One of our young men spotted a horse and rider headed this way. We've sent a squad to capture them."

"You may look up now, Sidian. Let me see your face."

Sidian did as he was told. He raised his head and forced himself to look into the queen's dispassionate and spiritless brown eyes. As usual, Queen Celesta had done her best to cover her pasty white face with makeup. Her ash blond hair was pinned in a bun behind her crown. She wore an iridescent silk dress, adorned with flashy jewels. The sight of her made Sidian sick, but his expression remained impassive so she wouldn't suspect how miserable he was. They stood there, staring at each other for what seemed like an eternity to Sidian.

Finally, the queen stopped scrutinizing him and shifted her attention to the picture in the portal. "Show me the intruders, General."

At Sidian's command, the clouds in the vortex swirled until a picture appeared of Iyon and Jen approaching the cliff. The queen tilted her head. Her eyes grew wide with excitement.

"Well, it looks like the plan is working after all."

"My Queen, is this the one you have been waiting for?" Sidian humbly asked.

"That girl, Sidian, is the Key Holder. I have something special in mind for her and her horse. She was poisoned in Shadow Earth and became trapped in the realm of Escapist, doomed to die there. But, thanks to my brilliance, she was freed and is on her way to us," Celesta said both devilishly and triumphantly.

She moved her hand over the picture of Iyon and Jen on the mysterious screen. As Celesta did this, the exquisite jewels on the sleeve of her gown shimmered in the light emitted by the magical picture. She paused for a moment and stared at Iyon, contemplating how she could harness his powers in order to make her stronger.

"We must not attack that creature, Sidian. He can easily wipe out the entire squad if he feels threatened in any way. Instead, we'll welcome the girl and her steed. Go to your troops and tell them to stand down. I want you to speak to our esteemed visitors yourself. See to it that they come peacefully and don't let them suspect anything. You must be honest and true, or he will read right through you. I'll give you further orders once they're secured inside my castle."

After adjusting the picture so that he could see his troops, the general bowed again to the queen, then disappeared into the portal to carry out her orders.

The queen was alone in the room. Once she saw that Sidian had joined his men, she spoke to her vortex, ordering it to show Iyon and Jen again. Running her hand over their image, she said, "Soon, Warrior Horse, you'll be mine to destroy or enslave as I please. And your rider, dear horse, will be mine forever." Celesta laughed wickedly as she left the room and headed to the banquet hall to make preparations for her doomed visitors.

....

The dungeon cell reeked of rotting flesh. In its center was what appeared to be a semi-transparent cocoon, large enough for a man. The Skeign proudly paraded John in while holding him fast with their tentacles. One of the Skeign approached the cocoon and pulled an iron lever with its claw. A rush of air escaped from the compartment as it slowly opened. Felonious entered the cell, carrying an iron helmet. He ordered the Skeign holding John's head to release its grip. Felonious took the helmet, which had the same pulsating powers as the tentacles of the Skeign, and placed it on John's head. This deadened John's mind and kept him from escaping.

Felonious snapped at the two Skeign to his right, "Put him in the chamber."

The two creatures jumped immediately into action. They lifted John up, and laid him inside the chamber. His hands were placed at his sides and cuffed down. His ankles were bound as well.

"Shut the chamber door. Initiate minimal life support. Work day and night until you break him. Our Master demands we find our enemies and the key."

The guard in charge of the interrogation responded with an affirmative growl. The sound of escaping air filled the room as the chamber door shut tight. Then Felonious and the other beasts stomped out of the room, leaving John alone with his interrogator. It circled around to the edge of John's prison where a small funnel protruded from the chamber. It opened the funnel, allowing John to get a breath of fresh air, but then blew its own breath inside. The smell was unbearably putrid. John's body jerked fiercely as he tried desperately to escape the odor, but there was nothing he could do. The creature laughed at John's futile efforts.

"My name is Dangor," it hissed. "And you will endure great suffering until you let me into your mind. You will show me where my enemies are hiding. And you will show me where you hid the key." The interrogator slid an especially thin tentacle down the shaft and it found its way to John's forehead. Once it was firmly planted in place, it ignited his body with impulses meant to directly affect the nervous system. John's screams of pain were heard from one side of the corridor to the other. The interrogator released John and left the room to attend to its other prisoners.

John was left alone with only his misery to keep him company. Amidst all the pain, he tried hard to focus someplace else, but his attempts proved ruthlessly futile. Evil attacked his mind, filling it with images of the Skeign. John did his best to block them out. Though he couldn't see a way out of this dreadful torturous chamber, he knew deep in his heart that there was still hope. And he would have to hang on to that hope with all his might, for if the Skeign found a way to break him, they would find a way to Jen. John wasn't going to let that happen, even if it killed him.

Chapter 26
The Invitation

Iyon stood in a valley, wondering where to look first for the chest. He sensed people approaching. "There's no need to go any further. They've found us and are coming our way," Iyon said.

Jen's heart pounded as she watched the people approaching. "I don't want to stay here. Something's wrong."

Iyon stood still, checking for any threats that the men might pose. "You mustn't be afraid, Jen. I'll protect you."

Iyon's eyes flared a dangerous dark blue. He stood motionlessly, his gem glowing and his tail of whips ready to attack. The men cautiously stood at attention. Sidian alone walked toward Iyon and Jen with his hands in the air. Then he stopped, knelt, and placed his hands on the bended knee.

"Warrior Horse and rider, please accept our most humble welcome, and forgive us for our suspicious approach. We are unaccustomed to receiving visitors. So when we do, we tend to be overly cautious. On behalf of Queen Celesta and the people of Eshron, we welcome you."

Iyon respectfully bowed his head as well, but remained on guard.

"Thank you for your warm welcome," Iyon said. "However, our stay here will be short."

Sidian stood up. "Understood, but please consider coming to our city for food and shelter. My queen would be so pleased to extend her greeting to you. In fact, I'm sure a meal is being prepared as we speak. We would be honored to have you join us."

Iyon cocked his head toward Jen and spoke quietly so that only she could hear him. "We can use this invitation to our advantage. It'll give me a chance to investigate the city and the castle to determine if she has the chest."

Jen felt uneasy about it, but decided to trust Iyon's judgment.

"Okay," she whispered warily.

"Lead on, soldier. We'll follow you," Iyon stated.

Sidian bowed once more. "Thank you. My queen will be most pleased."

The men walked in front, with Iyon and Jen following them. Apprehensive, Jen leaned forward and whispered again to Iyon, "Do you think this is a good idea? It just doesn't feel right."

Iyon nodded his head in agreement. "I know, but it gives us easy access to the queen." He snorted and threw back his head. "If anything goes wrong, I will take care of it."

"What if this whole thing is a big set up?"

"I've walked into traps purposely before; don't worry. Everything will be okay in the end. Besides, there's nothing they have here that can overtake me."

"Good to see your confidence is so high." Jen sighed and stared straight ahead as they followed the soldiers. The uncertainty of whether they were walking with a friend or an enemy frightened Jen horribly, but what choice did they have? The memory of the little girl in the peach garment saying, "Don't be afraid," flashed through her worried mind. Those encouraging words and Iyon's support gave Jen a little more ease. But still...

The men didn't bring Iyon and Jen through the vortex because they'd been strictly warned by the queen to keep its existence a secret. Instead, they zigzagged their way through a series of caves and tunnels until they arrived at the entrance to the city. The edges of Eshron were fortified by mile-high cliffs. It was here that the people of Eshron dwelt.

From within the caves, the soldiers let Iyon and Jen through several thick iron doors. When the last door opened they beheld the city of Eshron. It was as busy and bustling as Tolare. They paraded down the central road that led to the castle. People stopped their daily activities and lined the streets to greet the newcomers. It seemed odd to Jen that they would welcome strangers like this. She waved to the people or simply nodded her head in response to their greetings and many smiles. A number of people followed them along the dirt road. The high walls of a castle loomed ahead. When Iyon and Jen passed through a giant golden arch and entered a grassy field in front of the castle, the people stopped abruptly and returned to their routines.

Jen leaned over so she could get as close to Iyon's ear as possible. "Why do you think they stopped?"

"I sense there's magic in these fields, black magic, and even more in the castle."

"That makes me feel a whole lot better, Iyon," Jen said sarcastically as they walked through the open gates. Then they closed behind them.

Inside the castle, Jen dismounted Iyon. As they walked through the huge foyer, Iyon and Jen admired the mosaic tile floor. Stunning tapestries proudly concealed the rugged stone walls. An enormous shield depicting the family crest was suspended from the ceiling. While the other items were meticulously taken care of, the crest had been allowed to fall into disarray. The paint was so badly chipped that Iyon and Jen could barely make out the four-word motto: Liberty, Honesty, Loyalty, and Charity. The two of them exchanged glances.

The further they walked, the more people they saw, but, like the man leading them, they were silent. The women wore beautifully colored pastel saris decorated with shimmering gems and small particles of gold dust. Their heads and necks were delicately wrapped with matching scarves.

Iyon, Jen, and their guide proceeded down a hallway with walls made of shiny smooth stones. Every few feet, brass lanterns burned brightly, continuously lighting their way. The corridor led to a circular room with pillars around its circumference. At this point, the man in the toga said, "Please wait here." Then he bowed and hurried down the hall.

Intrigued by their surroundings, Iyon and Jen surveyed the room. Between each pair of pillars, except for one, were golden archways built into the walls. Each pillar was embedded with rare gems. In between the two pillars directly across from Jen and Iyon were eight stone steps. Plush pillows were scattered on the floor at the top of the steps. A pink and white satin curtain hung from the ceiling and draped down the center of the pillows.

The silhouette of a person stood behind it. A slender young woman stepped out from behind the curtain. She, too, was dressed in a silky sari with a matching veil concealing her face. But, unlike the other women, her sari was scarlet. It seemed obvious to Jen that she had a high rank among the others in the castle.

The young woman gracefully glided down the stairway and stood before them. Curtsying low to the ground, she said, "Warrior Horse and lady, welcome to our humble castle. I hope that you will find your stay most satisfying."

Iyon and Jen bowed as well. The young woman removed part of her veil and Jen was standing face to face with Zurina. Jen looked right at her but failed to recognize her. Since Jen was unconscious most of the time she was in the hospital, she was unaware that Zurina had helped to rescue her. Iyon, of course, knew who she was, but understood the danger of identifying her.

Zurina was unsure how the two of them would respond to her being in this world and serving the queen. And she certainly didn't want them to show any sign of knowing her, so right away she said, "I'm to escort you to a waiting room where you'll stay for a short time while the servants finish preparing a meal in your honor. Please, come this way."

Zurina approached a part of the wall that contained a golden arch but no opening. She walked straight through it and vanished before their eyes. Iyon and Jen stopped and wondered how this could've been done. She had vanished right through the stone wall. A few seconds later, Zurina came back through the wall.

"Don't be alarmed by the type of passageways and doors we have in parts of this castle. They're made of a special substance that you can walk right through, but yet looks completely solid. Now, please come with me."

Zurina once again disappeared into what looked like solid rock. Iyon poked his head in first and then went through with his whole body. Jen stepped up to the wall next. She tentatively reached out and swished her hand through it. It felt like water but left her hand dry when she pulled it out. After taking a deep breath, she jumped through the wall and bumped into Iyon, who was waiting for her on the other side.

"Come quickly, we must continue," Zurina said, her voice filled with anticipation and anxiety.

The three started down a hallway that had no visible doors, only archways every few yards. At the end of the hallway, Zurina paused for a moment before the last archway.

"This way please," she said and passed through another penetrable section of the wall. Iyon and Jen followed. They entered a rectangular room, wonderfully decorated with abstract pictures and sculptures that rested in concave sections along the walls. In the center of the room was an elegant gold-framed bed with an array of plush pillows. Next to the bed was a pedestal table made of ivory. The table was covered with sterling silver platters of tantalizing fruit. Jen noticed the mango-like birr she'd been given by Hope. She walked over to the platter and picked up a piece.

Zurina, who was still standing near the archway, turned her head and looked into Iyon's eyes. She wanted so badly to speak to him, to tell them of the trap, but knew the queen was watching her right now. Instead, she chose her words carefully.

"The queen hopes you'll enjoy the fruit as an appetizer before dinner. It's quite exquisite and will leave you content and relaxed."

Iyon caught her meaning. "Thank you, but we will wait until we meet your queen." He looked sternly over at Jen, who was getting ready to take a bite. She was quite puzzled by their conversation, but seeing the look on Iyon's face, she put the piece of fruit back where she found it.

"Well then, meet her, you definitely shall. I shall return for you shortly. Until then, please rest." She bowed and quietly left the room.

Iyon walked over to Jen and did a most peculiar action, but worked hard to make it seem as if he were just rubbing his head against Jen's back. He pressed against her back and let a beam of transparent power come forth from his eyes and enter into Jen, allowing Iyon to speak to her telepathically.

Don't look alarmed that you can hear me. In fact, laugh and ask what I'm doing so there are no suspicions. Jen obeyed. *The fruit is poisoned. I know the young woman who brought us to this room. She helped rescue you when you were trapped in the hospital and is a citizen of my home world.*

What's she doing here, Iyon?

I don't know.

Why is she working for the queen?

I don't think she is. She warned us not to eat the fruit and we are being watched.

Oh that's great!

At least we have an ally.

We think we have an ally.

I'm sure we do. Get some rest. I'll stand guard.

Okay.

Iyon moved his head away from Jen's back, breaking their telepathic connection. Jen walked to the bed and threw herself on the pillows. Weary from traveling, she let her mind drift off and was soon asleep.

Iyon stood over her and neighed gently and quietly. He didn't know what was going to happen, but he knew what lay ahead wouldn't be easy. Having an ally in the castle made him feel more at ease. Or was she on their side? Maybe she was planted in the dream world to help Jen escape because the queen wanted her for her own evil purposes. But, Zurina deliberately looked into Iyon's eyes to let him sense her true intentions.

No, Iyon concluded, *she is no enemy.*

No matter how the circumstances might appear, Iyon decided that he could rely on her. Then he closed his eyes and began formulating a plan.

Chapter 27
Flashbacks, Memories, and History

As soon as Zurina had carried out the queen's orders, she went on a little mission of her own. She quickened her pace down the hallway and through a couple of passageways until she reached the forbidden corridor. At the end, two heavily armed soldiers guarded the archway leading to the queen's library. They looked down at the shapely figure who quickly removed her veil so they could see her face. Then, without saying a word to Zurina, they stepped aside so she could enter the room.

As she slipped into the queen's private library, she remembered the way Iyon had stared into her eyes and hoped and prayed that he could see that she was a friend. Then her thoughts drifted back to the day her life changed forever.

....

It was a glorious day. Zurina had spent the afternoon picking berries in the nearby forest. She was walking down a hill on her way home when a powerful and chilling gust blew over the land. The sky changed from baby blue to venomous black as a horde of horrible creatures flew into the village and began their assault. People screamed and ran for their lives. Many were slain and others were bound and cast into iron-like nets. A few managed to escape to the hillside while others took off into the distant woods.

Zurina ran to a large mound of rocks and crouched down behind them.

She looked through a small hole and stared in terror as her village was destroyed. Suddenly, a Warrior Horse arrived and attacked the Skeign. Her heart raced, knowing it was Iyon! Fear turned to hope as she witnessed firsthand his incredible strength. Iyon's eyes emitted powerful lightning rays of power as he slew the Skeign. With his iron tail thrashing mightily and his eyes glowing fiercely, this valiant creature destroyed the enemy.

But the sky darkened again. More Skeign were headed their way. Sensing the approach of the enemy's reinforcements, Iyon urgently rescued as many villagers as he could. He slew the Skeign that was holding the iron-like nets full of prisoners. Then, grabbing the net in his own mouth, Iyon flew away with four more people on his back and several others hanging on to the outside of the net. As Iyon flew up to leave, he caught Zurina's scent from within the rocks and stared directly into the rocks. Their eyes met. He began to move in her direction, but large numbers of Skeign were flying from over the rocks. He had no choice. Iyon left and took the others to safety. The Skeign chased him, but Zurina could tell that he had a strong head start and would be okay. One of the survivors on Iyon's back looked like her younger sister, Tess. Zurina leaned her head against the rock. She closed her eyes and silently wept as the Skeign flew over her hiding place.

When Zurina opened her eyes and began to turn around; there, staring her in the face, was a man dressed in full armor. She startled and almost screamed, but he covered her mouth. Roughly spinning her to face back against the rock, he tightly bound her hands behind her back and gagged her. Then the soldier covered her head with a sack and carried her away.

. . . .

Many years before Zurina was captured and Tranquil Earth was attacked, the worlds were mostly free from the control of the Evil One. In the flourishing city of Eshron on Pure Earth lived a wise and noble queen named Miriam. Miriam wasn't the type to sit within the confines of her castle. Her adventurous spirit and love for her world led to many explorations. Her endless desire was to seek the unknown places of her world and see what great mysteries could be discovered.

But who knew that the greatest discovery would be found in the tunnels below her castle that led to deep unknown regions. On a day when she was wandering the many caves that surrounded her great city, she happened to find a most peculiar entrance. What was so special about it was never recorded but Miriam insisted on venturing in, and though her bodyguards urged against it, her persistence in the matter and her orders quickly shut down the argument. It curved and twisted deeper and deeper into the earth until she reached an open cavern with temple pillars built straight into the sides and ancient stone steps that led up to something emanating a faint glow.

On that day, Miriam climbed the steps and when she reached the top, there resting on a stone built table was a small wooden chest inlaid with gold. The unique lock was made of ivory. She could tell that no ordinary key would open this chest. When the guards went to pick it up for Miriam; their hands passed right through the chest as if it were nothing more than a mirage. All who witnessed this phenomenon were astounded. A chest that was there but utterly untouchable.

Perplexed, Miriam returned to the castle and sought the advice of her most trusted elders and advisors. They told her the tale of the River Chest that lived among the dimensions of the many worlds. Only a Key Holder had the power to handle the chest, but the identity of such a person was unknown to the elders. For days they debated amongst themselves the fate of the chest. Ultimately, the queen believed that the discovery had to be kept a secret. Though she herself didn't know the depth of the power within the chest, Miriam feared that if the wrong person found a way to open it, the results would change the balance of good and evil among the worlds.

Not too many days after the discovery of the chest, a foreigner was discovered in Eshron. He wandered out of the caves, was found by the patrol and taken before the queen. She marveled at the man for she could tell plainly by the clothes he was wearing that he was not of their world. His name was William, and he explained that he was a carpenter. Miriam was taken by the gentleness and humility of his spirit. He told Miriam that something had drawn him to her world, but how he had gotten to it, he was unsure. She offered for him to stay at the castle as she felt that he was peculiarly special in some way.

After several days, William desired to make the queen a gift to show his gratitude and so he asked for some wood and tools. He cut and fashioned a small wooden jewelry chest and presented it to the queen. Miriam was shocked when he gave her the gift, for it bore the uncanny resemblance of the mysterious chest that lay deep in the caverns somewhere below the city and castle. This prompted Miriam to ask her advisors if William should be allowed to see the chest. They all agreed, so they escorted William to the cave where it was located. Upon climbing the stairs and seeing the chest, he felt as if the sum of his whole life appeared before him and for that moment, everything made sense. He placed gentle hands, one on each side of the chest, and picked it up. A true Key Holder had found his way to the chest!

Miriam asked if he had the three-pronged key, but he did not. The chest was taken to the castle and brought to the library where another great wonder of their world was found, yet it too was mysteriously untouchable.

In the corner of the queen's private library was a giant globe of Pure Earth. It was made of gold. It towered almost nine feet high but it was not wide like a regular globe, but rather thin instead. It rested on a huge stand made of solid oak. Only by examining the globe closely would one notice that it had little hinges and a latch that could be opened. When opened, it revealed a portal to an unknown world. For as long as Eshron history had been recorded, it was a seemingly useless gateway since no one could come or go through it. The other side could be seen, but when a hand would try to press through, it was as tough as rock. If by some miracle the chest could be taken through this portal by the Key Holder, then it could be safely hidden from the evils of all the worlds forever.

When William saw the mystery of the portal in the golden globe, he set the chest down and walked toward the portal until he was standing next to Miriam, directly in front of the magical picture.

She put her hand up to it and pushed. All she could feel was rock. She turned and looked at William. He decided to take a step of faith and walked straight through. Instantly, he was on the other side. He turned and saw Miriam looking back at him from inside her library. He then stepped back through and was once again in the library.

She marveled, "All these years, dear William. All these years I thought it was but a silly trick or mirage. Now you have proven it is far more than that and real in every way."

"Ma'am," he said in his polite country manner, "all my life I've always known that I was meant to protect something special. I vow you this day. I will take the chest to this world and with my life I will protect it and keep it safe."

He then looked at the ground for a moment and acted as if there were more he wanted to say. But instead, he stared back at the queen, and nodded his head resolutely.

After a good night's rest and many provisions given by the queen, William picked up the River Chest and disappeared through the portal, never to be seen again.

The globe was sealed shut. Miriam and her advisors swore an oath not to tell anyone about the chest and what they had done with it. The queen alone had the responsibility to pass the secret down to her successor, as long as the new queen was pure of heart.

After many years, Miriam grew old and her daughter, Angelina, succeeded her to the throne. Angelina was found worthy, so she also became the keeper of the secret. In time, she married and gave birth to a baby girl, whom she and her husband named Celesta. When Celesta was two, her father died, leaving Angelina alone to raise the child and rule a kingdom. She raised the girl with firm discipline, doing her best to prepare her for the throne. Celesta wasn't one to receive discipline well, but as she grew older, she realized the need to play the role of the perfect daughter and thus gain the trust of her mother. Her scheme paid off. Believing that her daughter was pure of heart, Angelina told Celesta the secret of the chest when the girl turned eighteen. Strangely, a week after the birthday celebration, Angelina died of an unknown sickness, leaving her daughter to succeed her to the throne.

After the passing of her mother, Celesta realized how difficult it would be to actually get to the chest. Her mother had only told her part of the secret, saving the other half for when her daughter actually became queen. Celesta hadn't been told that the key to the chest was missing and that no one from her own world could enter the portal hidden in the mighty golden globe within the private library. So for a few years, she was stuck with royal duties that she wasn't ready for and absolutely despised.

During that time, the kingdom's crops failed and the people were on the brink of starvation, leaving Queen Celesta in a rather desperate circumstance. After the passing of many miserable months, Celesta demanded to be left alone one day. She grabbed a torch and sneaked through the castle, working her way down until she reached the lowest level. Cobwebs stuck to her dress and spiders crawled into their dark corners, hiding from the passing light as she walked down a hallway that had been vacated for many years. Stopping for a moment to catch her breath, she saw a line of cast-iron statues of mystical sea creatures that covered the full length of one side of the corridor. As Celesta strolled down the hallway studying the statues, she thought she heard the sound of footsteps approaching. Not wanting to be seen, she ducked behind one of the statues and put out her torch. She leaned up against what she thought was a solid stone wall. But instead, she fell right through it to the ground on the other side, dropping her torch and dirtying her blue satin dress. Grumbling, she clumsily picked herself up, smacking the dirt from her clothes. She found herself standing in a cave. To her right was a torch brightly burning in the middle of a fountain flowing with oil.

"How convenient."

Celesta picked up her own torch and relit it from the one in the fountain. Regaining her composure, she began to explore the cave. She walked slowly for quite a while until she entered a larger cave. It was full of hundreds of stalactites hanging from the ceiling and had mounds of stalagmites building up from the floor. Suddenly a wind extinguished Celesta's torch. The queen held her breath in the darkness. As her eyes adjusted, Celesta noticed a faint glow coming from the other end of the cave.

She cautiously approached the source of the dim light and beheld an incredible sight. There before her was a massive swirling vortex. The pointy tips of the stalagmites and stalactites had curled into and through this anomaly. The stalagmites and stalactites pulsated as if they were breathing and maybe even alive. Intrigued by this, Celesta carefully inched toward the spinning mass until she was standing directly in front of it. Despite the possible danger, Celesta had an overwhelming desire to touch the vortex. The moment she did, the swirling stopped. Everything within the vortex turned black. Then shapes began to form inside it. Soon stars appeared and a dark and eerie world, so unlike her own. Celesta stood there staring at the phenomenon, dumbfounded.

"Shadow Earth?" she murmured under her breath, remembering a world she'd heard about long ago from the elders.

With a deep yet alluring voice, the vortex spoke to her. "No, but I can show you Shadow Earth if you desire to see that wretched place."

Celesta jumped back and looked for a loose rock to use as a weapon.

"Don't be alarmed, I won't hurt you. Look! Here's the world you requested," said the mysterious vortex.

The clouds inside quickly dispersed and Shadow Earth appeared.

"If you're looking to take a trip, this isn't the place I'd suggest," said the voice.

Cold-hearted Celesta immediately began thinking of ways that she could use this vortex to her benefit.

"Can...can you show me a better world?" Celesta cunningly asked.

The image of Shadow Earth disappeared. The clouds within the swirling mass spun around and around like a hurricane. Pictured in the center of the vortex was a breathtakingly beautiful world.

Celesta took a few deep breaths, unable to find words to describe what was taking place before her.

"What are you?"

"Does it matter what I am? I'm inexplicable and unfathomable. I've been alone, trapped down here for ages and ages, waiting for someone to find me. You have found me. Don't abandon me like the one who came before you. I have the power to take you to places you haven't been and find you treasures beyond your wildest dreams. All I want in return is to be freed from this miserable prison. So let's make a pact with one another," the voice said enticingly.

A smile crept across Celesta's face as she realized that this new discovery could save her from all her troubles with the starving peasants.

"My name is Celesta, and I promise that you'll never be lonely again. I'll try to figure out a way to free you. What shall I call you?"

"What would you like to call me?"

Celesta thought for a moment and then said, "I'll call you Tor, after my deceased father. You speak of fortune; can you show me any riches in that beautiful world?" Celesta asked greedily.

"That world is known as Tranquil Earth and is full of wonderful gems."

The vortex showed the planet and zoomed in closer until a wooded area came into view. Nestled deep in the forest was a stone building with two barred windows near the top. Then the vortex proceeded to show Celesta exactly what was in there—a myriad of indescribably beautiful gems. It was a treasure that Celesta deeply desired to have for herself. The picture was so clear.

It seemed as if she could walk right into it.

"I wish I could be there right now," she said enviously.

"Is that truly what you want? I can take you there."

"You can? Do you mean to tell me that you can see into all known worlds and take me to them also?"

"Not every known world. There are a few mystical places that I cannot see into and others that I cannot enter. But that building in Tranquil Earth isn't one of them. The outside of the building is built with impenetrable material and only a Warrior Horse can open its doors, but I can bypass that and take you straight to the treasure."

Celesta extended her hand and dipped it into the swirling clouds. At that moment, a strange sensation swept through her body as Tor injected her with a minuscule portion of itself.

"Now you may enter. And whenever you want to come back, all you need to do is think of me and returning home, and I'll be there to take you away. I have now become a part of you."

"Do you require this of everyone who wants to travel through you?"

"No. I have given you a special connection to me. The other from long ago would not, but you were willing. You're free to enter whenever you're ready."

"Well, their loss, my gain."

Celesta gingerly stepped into Tor. It was surprisingly simple, nothing more than walking through a doorway. Once inside the building, she quickly surveyed the walls and saw, bolted on them, a few metal hooks holding cloth bags. Hastily snatching an empty one off a hook, she went over to the mountain of gems and eagerly filled the bag until it was overflowing. Then she thought of going home, and Tor instantly appeared. Celesta stepped into the vortex and was gone. When she arrived on the other side, she yelled, "Close!" It obeyed.

"In the future, Celesta, you won't need to say that. Thanks to you, I can now close my passageways immediately and only let through whom I want to let through."

As she looked into the bag of glittering gems she had just stolen, a greedy grin spread across Celesta's face.

Over the next couple of weeks, Celesta devised a series of tests to see which of her soldiers were willing to get their hands dirty for a little extra money, and which ones weren't. The ones who weren't were sent away on assignments far from the castle. She bought the loyalty of over two hundred soldiers and a few government officials who would do anything for money and power.

With the help of Tor, the queen sent her soldiers on missions to steal grain from other worlds, thereby providing an abundance of food for the starving peasants of Eshron. Since she ended the famine, her subjects were deceived into thinking that she cared about them and thus became great in their eyes.

Celesta continued using Tor for personal gain. It showed her troops when to access the temples and museums of other worlds without being noticed. The soldiers stole precious artifacts from one world, gems from another, and captured exotic animals from other worlds. The creatures were caged in a zoo built for the queen in her garden behind the castle. Looking down at her zoo from her window, she laughed maniacally.

....

One day when Celesta was alone with Tor, she remembered that she still needed the missing key to the chest. With all the time she'd spent stealing from other worlds, she'd temporarily forgotten about it. "Find me the world that has the key to the River Chest," she demanded.

Tor searched for a number of days until it finally came across the key in Shadow Earth and showed it to Celesta. Ignoring Tor's advice to stay away from that place, Celesta walked through and landed in a temple where hideous creatures were bowing down to a dragon that dwelt within a black vortex. In front of this vortex stood a stone pedestal on which rested a golden three-pronged key. Celesta couldn't believe her eyes.

Felonious, the lieutenant of the Skeign in Shadow Earth, looked up and growled viciously at the intruder. Celesta was frightened, but her greed exceeded her fear. She reached out and tried to steal the key, but her hand passed right through it. She paused in surprise, and Felonious whipped his tentacles around her neck and yanked her closer to himself. He snarled and held her head in front of his face.

With drool dripping from his fangs, he sneered, "Foolish human! Only a Key Holder from Tranquil Earth can pick that up." He threw Celesta into the air and she landed on the temple's stone floor. Aching all over, she struggled to remain conscious.

Felonious snapped his tail and pounced toward his victim. The legion watched, roaring in glee at the entertainment.

"Time for you to die!"

"Tor, get me out of here!"

Felonious swung his razor sharp claws at her face, but he was too late.

All he hit was thin air. Celesta was gone!

Tor had swept her up from Shadow Earth and brought her home. Celesta sat down on the rocky cave ground, pressed her knees against her chest, and stared at the mysterious swirling mass, waiting to see if Felonious would follow her. Nothing happened.

Finally, Tor spoke. "That was Felonious, the lieutenant of the creatures called the Skeign in Shadow Earth. He won't be able to come through me, Celesta, no matter how hard he may want to. He does not know me. But I would suggest that you not go there again."

"Agreed. I know where the chest is, I just saw where the key is and now, thanks to Felonious, I know that a Key Holder is in Tranquil Earth. I need to find that person, but how?" Celesta needed time to devise a plan.

....

After receiving Felonious' report of the mysterious woman attempting to obtain the key, Dolorous realized that now others knew of its location.

"If a Key Holder succeeds in getting that key and finding the chest, who knows what power could be released against us?"

"What would you have me do, General?" Felonious asked, trying hard to appease his superior.

"Guard the key with your life."

"Yes, General."

"See that you do because if anything happens to it, you'll suffer the consequences."

"I will not fail you," Felonious said, bowing.

Dolorous approached the Master with a vicious idea. War would be waged on Tranquil Earth and all its citizens would be captured or killed. That would eliminate the threat of the Key Holder coming from that world altogether. Thus came the fateful day that Tran was taken over.

....

When Tor told Celesta that Tran was being attacked by Dolorous and the Skeign, she took the opportunity to put her own plan into action. She mobilized and ordered her troops to kidnap citizens throughout Tranquil Earth to be used as servants, tending to all the chores of the castle and the zoo. However, her real reason for capturing these people was to find a Key Holder. While Dolorous and the people of Tran were engaged in battle, Celesta's troops were free to carry out their orders without being noticed.

Celesta became more and more obsessed with finding a Key Holder before Dolorous and the Skeign did. She thoroughly interrogated the prisoners to see if they knew the identity of a Key Holder. When she was convinced they didn't know anything, she made them servants. She ordered her troops to imprison them in the dungeon cells below the castle. And when all the cells were filled, she used the caves below the dungeons as well to hold more captives.

Frustrated that she couldn't get any answers, Celesta resorted to sorcery. She learned about the spells from books on incantations and black magic that she'd stolen from one of the darker worlds. By studying hard, she quickly learned the ways of evil, practicing many of the spells on her prisoners. But she still couldn't find a Key Holder.

In the meantime, Celesta brought ten women from the dungeon to learn how to wait on her hand and foot. These women were given colorful saris, collars and golden chains to wear instead of iron ones. They stood in total silence as the queen came to examine each one. Zurina was among them. While she'd been held in the dungeon, she'd devised a deceptive plan of her own in hopes that one day the opportunity to carry it out would arise.

When the queen came to stand before her, Zurina fell to the ground and kissed the queen's feet.

"My mistress, forgive this servant for speaking. I can see that you're exceptionally powerful. The most important thing to me is being on the winning side. Allow me to help you conquer other worlds. I'll show you how valuable I can be," Zurina said as she remained at the queen's feet.

The queen was outraged that Zurina dared to move and speak in her presence.

"Sidian! Wasn't this slave trained to speak only when spoken to?" she said disgustedly.

"Yes, my Queen," he humbly replied.

"Apparently, she hasn't learned her lesson yet. Take her back to the dungeon."

"Yes, my Queen."

Sidian grabbed Zurina's collar chain and jerked her to her feet. Celesta searched Zurina's eyes for any guile, but could find none. So she changed her mind and decided on a punishment that would be both beneficial and entertaining.

"Wait a minute, Sidian. Chain her to the floor before my throne instead."

Celesta took Zurina's chin, shook it, and then released it with a rough snap. "We'll soon find out if you're lying to me or not."

The next couple of months were completely agonizing for Zurina. The queen cast a mute spell on her as a lesson to the others. That way no one ever spoke again without the queen's permission.

Celesta made Zurina her personal slave, which meant she had to be ready for service before the queen arose, and wait on her until the queen retired at night. Zurina was forced to remain at Celesta's side, doing whatever was demanded until the girl would collapse from sheer physical exhaustion. Then she was dragged to a room concealed by a secret door next to the queen's bedroom. The hidden room's only light came from a single candle on a small wooden table. Suspended in midair in the center of the room was a circular cage with bars made of iron. Every night, the guards would lower the cage to the ground, unlock the door, and shove Zurina in. After locking her up and raising the cage, they left her alone for a few hours with nothing but a small ripped up mattress to sleep on. Then the process began again.

It was during those few hours of rest that Zurina silently cried and meditated on how she could find a way into the queen's confidence. One day she would make the queen pay for all her treachery.

Chapter 28
Fake Loyalty

After Zurina lived under those conditions for two months, the queen made a decision. While sitting on her throne, she said to Zurina, "Come and kneel before your Queen."

Zurina immediately obeyed. She came and knelt before Celesta and then bowed until her forehead touched the ground.

"Now I'm going to test your profession of loyalty. I will release you from the mute spell for one minute. If I decide that what you have to say is worthless I will cast the spell on you for the rest of your days and send you to the dungeon. Now, begin speaking."

The queen smirked at Zurina, thinking that nothing the girl could say would save her from her fate.

"My Queen, I'll prove to you that I'm your most loyal subject. I have thought of a way for a Key Holder to end up in your palace without any effort on your part."

Zurina spoke no more. She waited in great anticipation to see if the queen would bite at her offer.

Celesta's eyes lit up. She was intrigued by the possibility that this girl might be useful to her after all. Not wanting to seem too anxious, Celesta said, "Go ahead and stand up, you drudge, and tell me your name."

Zurina raised her head. "My name is Zurina, and it will be my pleasure, my Queen, to tell you of my plan."

The queen arose from her throne and spoke to one of her attendants. "Bring her and follow me."

The guard bowed his head and obeyed. He followed at a respectful distance and took Zurina down the forbidden corridor that led to the queen's private library. As soon as they arrived at the entrance, which looked like an ordinary wall despite the golden archway, the queen motioned for the guard to stop and said coldly, "This is as far as you need to go. I'll take her from here." He bowed his head, held out his hand so she could take the lead chain and left them.

Once inside the library, Celesta led Zurina to the center of the room. She circled the young woman like a shark circling its prey. Zurina eyed the walls that were covered with shelves, filled with statues and books. Then she saw a large globe in the far corner of the room. Zurina lowered her head and stood silently, waiting patiently for permission to speak.

"I've made sure these past couple of months that you were given the most degrading treatment possible. That way, if there was any deceit within you, I'd see it in your eyes," said Celesta. She stopped in front of Zurina for a moment. "Look up and show me your eyes again." Zurina looked up and stared confidently into the eyes of the queen. Celesta was impressed by Zurina's demeanor.

"Hmm, I haven't seen what I thought I would. If your plan to find a Key Holder succeeds, then I give you my word to make you as great, powerful, and rich as any servant could ever dream of becoming. Now, tell me about this plan of yours."

Finally! All of Zurina's horrific pain and misery would now pay off. Zurina mustered up great excitement within her as she would finally have the chance to tell the witch her great plan that she hoped would ultimately be the queen's downfall. She took a deep breath and began.

"You need the key, a Key Holder, and the chest. Since you know the key is in Shadow Earth, you must first watch the comings and goings there. That way you'll know when the key has been taken. Let them do the dirty work that needs to be done on Shadow Earth. Watch and be entertained. You also know that there's a Key Holder in Tranquil Earth, so you should send someone who is pure of heart, innocent, and unknowing of our plan there to spread the word that the legendary River Chest is being kept here in Eshron. The news will draw that Key Holder here with the key. Be forewarned that a powerful Warrior Horse might accompany this person. But with your black magic, you, my Queen, will defeat him. Then all you have to do is send that Key Holder to retrieve the River Chest and you'll have everything you need to become the most powerful ruler of all the worlds of Earth."

The queen smiled devilishly. She was so hung up on her thirst for power; Zurina was easily able to win her over with the simple temptation of more power and wealth.

"We will keep your lovely plan to ourselves," Celesta said as she wandered toward the globe. "I know someone who's gullible and naïve who we can put in a point of danger, have him whisked away to this other world. He'll sell the story with no ill intentions in his heart. They won't know the difference. Just leave the rest to me."

She wandered around the golden globe while letting her mind roll with her new and exciting sadistic plan.

Jordan is a naïve young man. I'll let the elders tell him the stories of the chest. Then send him on his way. By the time he's rescued, he won't be able to keep his mouth shut about it. And then the Key Holder will be lured right into my trap.

Celesta turned and looked approvingly at Zurina. "My other servants aren't as crafty as you. I like your style. I need the guards and officials for now, but when I obtain access to the chest, you'll be my second in command if you continue to be loyal to me."

Zurina smiled. "That's more than I could ever have hoped for, my Queen. Tell me what I need to do to continue to prove my loyalty."

Celesta thought for a moment. "All right. You can start by finding someone from your own world to replace you as my servant. I also want to know if there are any hidden treasures in Tranquil Earth that we haven't found yet. Bring me the treasures from your own world, and then I will know that I can fully trust you."

Brokenhearted, yet forbidding herself to show it, Zurina responded, "I said anything, dear Queen. You want a new personal servant; I'll find one for you. You want treasure from my world; I'll get it for you. Whatever you want, I'll seek to fulfill. Let me be more than a servant in your eyes."

"We'll see about that. You will, at times, be allowed to leave the castle, accompanied, of course, by my trusted guards. But don't ever forget, you belong to me."

"There will come a day," Zurina said solemnly, "when you'll trust me enough not to have to worry about my betraying you."

"Let's hope so. We must go. There's much work to be done."

From that day on, Zurina slowly and methodically gained the trust of the queen. She eventually became Celesta's personal assistant, having the run of the castle and even the slaves and eventually was given the right to leave the castle unaccompanied.

Chapter 29
Strange Happenings

Zurina stopped reminiscing as she entered the queen's private library. She walked across the room to a wheeled serving cart that held a large metal strongbox. Locked inside the strongbox was a magical vine that had been taken from the jungle of Untamed Earth, a world full of the most extraordinary creatures and devoid of human life.

Several months ago while exploring this unknown dimension, Celesta's guards found themselves deep inside the mysterious jungle. So fascinated were they by the strangeness of their surroundings, the soldiers failed to pay attention to the seemingly ordinary vines that hung down from the branches of the trees. Without warning, one of the vines dropped down and landed on the head of one of the soldiers. At first, the others laughed, but all laughter stopped when the vine slithered down the side of the soldier's face and coiled around his neck and body. Suddenly, the jungle came alive with hundreds of hissing, creeping vines. The guards shrieked and bolted for their exit as vines dropped down on them. They ran and jumped through Tor. The guard who was originally attacked escaped through the vortex as well, with the vine still coiled around his neck and chest.

Celesta was nearby when the men returned in a frenzy. They were trying desperately to free their comrade from the vice-like grip of the hissing vine, but all their efforts were in vain. Making use of her knowledge of black magic, Celesta cast several sleep spells on the vine before the men were finally able to work it off the soldier. Despite the soldiers' pleas to send this vile plant creature back to where it came from, Celesta decided otherwise. Instead, she had the vine locked in a metal strongbox until she could discover how to control it. After a month of hopeless attempts to control it through the use of spells, or to befriend it, Celesta gave up and planned to have it destroyed.

Zurina was intrigued by this wild vine and decided to tame it, in hopes of impressing Celesta. She began experimenting with different liquids to feed it and formulated a mixture of juices, freshly squeezed from the finest fruits found in Eshron. Opening the small peep hole at the top of the strongbox, she took the juice and poured it in. To her surprise, the creature stopped banging against the sides of its prison and began purring. She presented the vine to the queen, who was delighted to see that this newly formulated elixir subdued it. Before long the vine became addicted to the elixir, so Celesta used it as a means of controlling the vine to do her bidding.

....

Iyon opened his eyes and looked at Jen lying on the bed, still sound asleep. Knowing that he couldn't tell her his plan, he worried about Jen's ability to have complete faith in him. Suddenly, he sensed a familiar presence, but was unable to detect who or what it was. Fearful of leaving Jen alone, he went to the window in hopes of discovering its whereabouts. After a few moments, Iyon was no longer able to sense the presence. It had faded away, leaving him baffled.

....

John fought for every breath of air as he tried to fill his lungs. It was exhausting work. The chamber in which he was trapped was so hot his clothes were drenched in sweat. He was tired and thirsty. His heart pounded in terror as he heard the interrogator coming back into the cell. It growled under its breath, opened the funnel and breathed into it, sending

John into convulsions as he tried to escape the smell. Then it closed the funnel again, forcing John to suffer a while longer.

Finally, the creature opened the funnel and spoke to him. "How much longer do you think you can resist me? Give me what I want and all your pain will be ended."

The Skeign slid one of its tentacles down the funnel, caressed John's forehead, and said in an enticing manner, "Let me in, John. Let me into your thoughts."

The voice was soothing, but John knew better. He could feel the presence of evil knocking on the door of his mind, wanting to come in, so he resisted with all of his might.

The interrogator growled and set John's body into shock as it pulsated with the most gruesome pain from the tentacle. Then it removed the tentacle and breathed into the funnel. It mattered little to the Skeign how often this process was repeated. Eventually, John would become too exhausted to fight anymore. It was only a matter of time.

Chapter 30
The Sign of the Doves

Zurina left the queen's library, pushing the cart that held the strongbox. On her way to the banquet hall, she briefly stopped at her room. Next to the bed stood a wicker cage housing a pair of doves. The doves had been a gift to her from Rozor, who, like her, realized that the wicked queen needed to be removed from power. Whenever the queen had sent her alone on errands, Zurina had found ways to communicate with trustworthy townspeople. In time, she developed her own band of followers who promised to fight against the queen when the doves were released. This sign of the doves would mean only one thing: it's time.

Zurina wheeled the cart into her room and went over to the doves. Tears formed in her eyes as she opened the cage and let them climb onto her hand. Saying a quiet prayer that they would come through for her, Zurina walked to the window and released them in the air.

"Go," she whispered. "Go find Rozor."

Realizing that there was much to do, Zurina left the window, quickly changed into her dinner gown, walked to the table next to her bed, opened a secret compartment under the table top, and pulled out a vial. She carefully placed the vial inside a pocket well hidden in the folds of her dress and departed from the room with the strongbox.

Worried that the queen would notice her absence, Zurina quickly wheeled the strongbox into the banquet hall. The queen, however, had no idea how long Zurina was gone. She was far too busy barking out orders at the servants about setting the table. Though she had no intention of actually sitting down and eating with Iyon and Jen, Celesta at least wanted a good show.

Zurina approached the queen, curtsied and said, "Here's what you desired, my Queen."

"Put it against the wall," Celesta commanded, looking around to make sure everything was the way she wanted it.

Zurina bowed and did as she was told.

"Yes, everything is coming together perfectly. It's time. Zurina, go and bring our guests to the hall now. I suspect they didn't recognize you, right?"

Zurina bowed her head again. "No, they didn't see me in the previous world. I kept my distance from them. How will Iyon be handled, my Queen?" she asked, wanting to change the subject.

"How dare you ask me such a question! Have you forgotten your place?" Celesta snapped.

"I'm sorry, my Queen, for overstepping my ground. I just want everything to go well for you."

"While you were away taking care of what you were expected to do in that dream realm, I have been busy." Although Celesta had no intention of keeping any of her promises to Zurina once she gained possession of the chest, for now, she still needed her help. So Celesta regained her composure and spoke more calmly to her. "Look, there are some things I plan that I don't want to burden you with. Go and bring Iyon and the girl to me, and I'll handle them."

"Yes, my Queen." Zurina about faced, hurried out of the banquet hall, and went straight to where Iyon and Jen were staying. With every step, she worried about the plan that Celesta had kept from her. For the sake of Eshron and all the other worlds of Earth that still remained free, Zurina knew that her own plan to defeat the queen must not fail.

Chapter 31
It's time

"Jen, wake up," Iyon said softly. "Jen," he called again and nudged her with his head.

Jen stretched, groaned, and then said, "What is it, Iyon?"

"It's time."

Jen immediately sat up. "Do you have a plan?"

"Yes," was all he said.

Before Jen could question Iyon further, Zurina walked in. She remained at the door and spoke urgently. "The banquet has been prepared and the queen requests that you come at once." They all looked at one another, but knew they couldn't speak out loud for fear of the walls having ears. Jen glanced nervously at Iyon, but he nudged her toward the door.

As they were leaving the room, Iyon pressed his head against Jen's back so that he could communicate with her telepathically.

Remember what I said. We can trust Zurina.

Then he lifted his head, separating his connection with Jen.

I'm petrified and I don't know what I'm getting myself into. I wish you could hear my thoughts now, Iyon. I wish you could coach me through this whole thing. Can you? Can you hear me?

There was nothing.

That's okay. I trust you, no matter what. And I trust your judgment about Zurina.

Iyon and Jen followed Zurina down the corridor until they reached the banquet hall, a long, narrow, windowless room that had no other visible doors. Shimmering gems, embossed in the ceiling, illuminated the room. The table was set with twenty chairs on each side. All plates, silverware and goblets were golden, encrusted with rubies, emeralds, and other tantalizing gems. At the end of the table in her own special chair sat the queen. She rose and smiled at her long awaited guests. Seeing the table set for forty guests, Iyon thought it strange that he, Jen, Zurina, Queen Celesta, and a servant girl were the only ones in the room. Every fiber within him was telling him how dangerous of a game he was playing as he knowingly walked into a trap. But this wasn't the first time Iyon had done this. He was confident that there was nothing that this woman could do against him.

Celesta raised her hand and gestured for them to come closer. "Welcome, welcome to my humble castle. So glad you could come. Zurina, please escort Tabitha to the kitchen. I'll meet up with you a little later."

Zurina motioned to the servant girl to follow her out of the room, leaving Iyon and Jen alone with the queen.

Iyon's muscles tensed as his eyes glared dark blue. The sound of the liar's words caused a shiver down his back. He detected only evil from Celesta.

Immediately after Zurina left, objects near the ceiling and along the sides of the walls caught Iyon's attention, and for a moment, he lost focus on the queen. There, in little individual niches, were precious statues from the museum of Tran. Iyon's nostrils flared in anger. The queen smiled, knowing that he was appalled to see the stolen artifacts.

"Don't bother us with your hospitality. I can sense the treachery and deception within you," Iyon said irately.

The queen maintained her composure, for she was confident in her plan.

"Queen Celesta to you, horse. You seem bothered. Are you all right?" she mocked.

Her mockery caused Iyon to flare all the more. He stomped his foot on the ground, causing the entire room to vibrate. After Jen regained her own footing, she straddled his back, leaned forward, and whispered, "You know she's just playing you, Iyon."

He made no effort to control his anger and snapped at the arrogant witch queen before him. "We'll keep our visit brief. You obviously know why I have come. When I find what I am looking for, I will take it along with all that you have stolen from Tran. Then I'll see to it that you're punished for all crimes that you have committed."

Jen was almost shaking while sitting on Iyon. He was caught off guard and Jen could sense evil lurking all around them now.

"Iyon, we need to get out of here."

Ignoring her, Iyon slammed his hoof on the ground again.

"What are you doing?" Jen whispered nervously.

"Well, then I guess this means dinner is off," the queen said casually. "What a shame. I had a splendid meal planned for you. Oh well." The queen raised her hand and snapped her fingers.

....

Zurina raced through the halls, slipping through unseen doorways, trying desperately to reach her destination. But as she turned the final corner, she was snatched by two men. One covered her mouth while the other bear hugged her from behind. The one that covered her mouth was trying to calm her as she frantically fought to break free. With his other hand, the soldier in front removed his helmet and signaled his comrade to release her.

"Jared!" Zurina whispered. She embraced him, then quickly let go.

"This is Taq," said Jared, pointing to the lanky man standing beside him.

Zurina nodded to Taq, then glanced back at Jared. "I have no idea how you pulled this off, but your timing is perfect. Put your helmet back on and follow me."

Zurina knew that the queen was busy with Iyon and Jen, but she feared the queen's soldiers could be watching them through Tor. However, this was a risk she was going to have to take, and Tor would probably have his vision glued to the main attraction by now.

....

From behind the magical walls of the banquet hall, a black stallion bounded into the room. Iyon reared up on his hind legs in shock at the sight of another Warrior Horse. Staring at his own kind face to face was bittersweet for him. He knew now this was what he had sensed earlier—the familiarity, yet not what it should be. No Warrior Horse could ever be black.

The eyes of the black horse blazed metallic orange as he stood ready to battle Iyon.

Iyon was in shock but geared up for the unimaginable. His heart pounded and broke.

The queen calmly said to her stallion, "Malum, it's time."

With tremendous force, the creature reared up on his hind legs. He tilted his head back and then thrust it forward, releasing all his power through his eyes and catching Iyon by utter surprise at the strength of his power. Iyon forced a counter-attack with his own bolt of energy, but not as powerful as his foe. Jen's lips quivered as she knew her comrade and friend faulted in his attack against one of his own. For her, a dreadful fate came over them and she knew there was nothing she could do.

"Iyon! You must fight him!" was all she could think of to say.

The queen muttered a spell under her breath, causing the walls on the sides of the banquet hall to vanish. Iyon and Jen found themselves completely surrounded by soldiers.

"Now!" Celesta yelled.

Iyon was trying to fight off Malum. Power exploded from Iyon's eyes, and Malum's, the flow clashing in between them. Soldiers bombarded Iyon with laser blasts and whipped him with chains and cords covered in spikes with poison-covered tips meant to weaken him. One chain was thrown around Jen's arms and chest, yanking right off of Iyon's back. While Malum kept his position against Iyon, rendering him useless against the soldiers, they advanced their attack and worked quickly, using the chains to bind Iyon's front hooves together and then his back hooves together. Jen screamed and watched in horror as the great Warrior Horse crashed to the ground. Malum continued his ruthless attack until his rays pressed up against Iyon's eyes. Iyon groaned under the force of the black stallion who was more powerful than he.

The queen signaled Sidian, who left the room and returned shortly, carrying an ivory container. He approached the queen, bowed, and set the container at her feet. Magically, the lid lifted off and out floated a metallic mask in the shape of a horse's head. Celesta motioned with her hands, causing the mask to fly straight toward Iyon's face.

"Move aside now, Malum," she commanded.

Using the laser beams from his eyes, Malum continued to pin Iyon down until he was sure that Iyon was too weak to fight back. Then Malum shifted the rays and pressed it against Iyon's chest with a direct shot at his heart if need be. Knowing that the blast could kill him, Iyon surrendered.

The queen motioned again. This time the mask magically wrapped itself around Iyon's entire face, even his eyes. Having achieved this victory, the queen proudly stood over him and locked the mask into place. As soon as the key clicked, it instantly liquefied, covering the lock and creating a permanent prison of darkness for Iyon.

Jen screamed and tried to jerk away from the soldier's grasp. "No! Let him go!"

Celesta pointed at Jen and said, "And now to deal with you." Then, whirling around to face Sidian, she ordered, "The strongbox, bring it to me!"

Sidian turned and walked toward the strongbox. The extent of the queen's cruelty shook his inner core to the point where he could take it no more. He knew the queen's plan and there was only one way to stop it. Destroy what was in that box. Making up his mind no matter the consequences, he pulled out his laser gun and attempted to destroy the box and the vine inside it. One of the soldiers, who was jealous of the general and eager to climb up the ranks immediately, reacted and shot the gun out of Sidian's hands before he could completely destroy the box.

"Seize him!"

Sidian was tackled to the ground by several of his own men and tightly chained and shackled.

"Take that traitorous rat to the lowest part of the dungeon, hang him from the rafters and leave him to rot!"

"Yes, my Queen, with pleasure." They roughly yanked their former commander and dragged him away.

Celesta looked at the man who'd thwarted Sidian's efforts and said, "You there, you will take his place. What's your name?"

"Dange," the young man proudly said.

"Bring me the strongbox."

The newly promoted soldier hurriedly did what the queen requested. When he returned, he proudly positioned himself where Sidian used to stand. Celesta unhooked the latch, and the lid flew open. The vine leaped out and coiled like a snake in front of Celesta.

"Go to the girl and imprison her."

Jen tried in vain to free herself from the soldier's firm grip as the vine slithered in her direction. It stood up like a cobra and hissed in her face. She jerked her head away, completely horrified, while the vine deftly wrapped around her hands, feet, and neck, then the soldiers laughed and let go of her.

"Well, that was easy. Guards, take Iyon to the cell Malum and I prepared for him. Keep him chained." Then, looking at Jen, she added, "And soon, my Key Holder, you'll see what I have in store for you." Celesta paused, walked over to Jen, and whispered in her ear, "You see, the vine that you now wear will make you obey every command I give you."

Jen gasped in both terror and disbelief as the queen spoke. Celesta snatched a laser gun from one of the guards and held it in front of her.

"Don't believe me? Watch this. Take this gun from my hand."

Jen tried to resist, but it was impossible. The vine forced her hand to grasp the gun. Tears of frustration streamed down her face as she realized that she was at the mercy of a witch that can control her every move.

"Lift up the gun and point it at your precious Iyon."

She cried out in defeat, "Please don't make me do this!"

Knowing that she had Jen right where she wanted her, Celesta smiled evilly, placed her finger on the barrel of the gun, and pushed it away from Iyon.

"I won't make you kill him, not unless you misbehave," Celesta said. Then, looking down on Iyon, she continued, "Besides, once his power is taken, he'll make a great addition to the zoo I've created. A life in a small cage living blind will be perfect for him." Turning to Jen, she commanded, "Give me the gun and follow me." The vine forced Jen's body to obey.

The guards brought in a thick leather harness and wrapped it around Malum's neck and chest. Then they grabbed the chains holding Iyon and attached them to the harness.

"All secure, Malum," one of the men said.

Accompanied by twenty armed soldiers, Malum dragged Iyon to the dungeon.

....

With Jared and Taq close behind her, Zurina ran through a hidden underground tunnel. They dodged roots dangling from the ceiling of the cave, and, at times, jumped over large rocks blocking their way. The three stopped short in front of a metallic door.

Zurina said, "You have to figure out how to open this door, Jared, and someone will be on the other side to tell you what to do from there. I must go before the queen notices I'm gone."

Jared responded, "What do we do if no one is there?"

Zurina was already running off, but yelled back to them, "They'll be there!"

Jared looked at Taq, who was studying the steel door quizzically. In the center was a wheel that controlled three metal bars sealing the door. On impulse, Taq removed his weapon from inside his armor.

"Wait," Jared quickly commanded. "Zurina said that help should be on the other side. You might kill someone by mistake."

"You're right," Taq said, lowering his weapon and putting it away.

They could see that the wheel needed to be turned in order to unlock the door.

"Let's get started," Jared said.

....

While Celesta and Jen were heading to the queen's library, Zurina was frantically crawling through a ventilation shaft in an effort to get there first. She was moving so fast that when she got to the library, she fell out of the vent, landing on her back. As she struggled to get to her feet, she stepped on her dinner gown, and the vial she'd been carrying in the inside pocket fell to the ground.

Oh no!

She scrambled to the vial and picked it up ever so gently to see if it had cracked. Breathing a sigh of relief that it was still intact, Zurina carefully put it back in her pocket, stood up straight, and wiped herself off. She hurried to the marble table next to the queen's favorite fruit, grapes grown in the upper hills of Eshron. All she needed to do now was to wait for the right time to pour the elixir onto the grapes.

....

Jen followed Celesta down the corridor that led to the queen's private library. As they walked, Celesta boasted, "I have a servant who came up with a most ingenious plan to lure a Key Holder to Eshron. She suggested that we watch the comings and goings in Shadow Earth because that's where the key was located. Once we discovered that your father was a Key Holder, we watched him closely but didn't intervene. However, there were complications. Originally, we thought we could kidnap him once he had the key, but then we lost track of him. Then you came along and, to our surprise, we learned you were also a Key Holder, so we kept track of you. We worried we'd lose you when you were poisoned by the Skeign. Later, you ended up in the realm of Escapist. Since we anticipated this, we took the necessary precautions. I had my servant work herself into Escapist's domain before you arrived there. I still don't know how she helped to free you from that place. I haven't had time to hear her story, but I look forward to it when this is all over."

You know nothing of who Zurina really is, thought Jen with a sweet taste of revenge in her heart. A human with no compassion is not a human, but a monster. The sooner this woman is brought down the better! And Jen couldn't wait, yet with her now as the queen's puppet, and Iyon locked in the dungeon, she did not see a way. Hope fled from her.

Celesta and Jen continued to the end of the corridor. Jen listened in silence as Celesta went on and on about her plan to rule once she gained access to the great power she assumed was in the chest. Jen hoped that Zurina would come up with something to thwart the evil queen.

They entered the library and found Zurina, kneeling motionless as a statue, next to the queen's chair.

....

Jared and Taq strained their muscles trying to open the door. Stopping for a minute to catch his breath, Taq looked questioningly at Jared. "How was Zurina planning to do this all by herself? Did she know we were coming? I hope this isn't a trap."

Wanting to keep up their morale despite his inner doubt, Jared said, "Iyon trusts her. I'm not going to cross that road with him again."

At long last, they succeeded in turning the wheel that removed the metal bars. Covered in perspiration, they stood back as the door was now being pushed open from the outside.

Jared looked at Taq, but didn't say anything. Not knowing if the people on the other side were friends or foes, the two pulled out their weapons and prepared themselves for the worst.

A man's head poked through the opening. He had a pointed nose and wore a cap flat to his head that covered his ears. A shock of red hair stuck out the front of the cap and covered his forehead. "Hello there. You must be Jared. Name's Rozor. Zurina told me you'd be here," he said, grinning.

Rozor had originally been reluctant to help fight Celesta as his wife had just given birth to their fourth child. But his wife assured him that it was the right thing to do. She knew how much her husband loved his family and all the people of Eshron. Rozor would do whatever he could to bring peace and prosperity to their land. After joining the rebellion, it wasn't long before others looked beyond his appearance and, recognizing his good qualities, made him their leader.

Jared and Taq glanced at each other and then back at the funny-looking man. Seeing that Rozor was a friend, they put away their guns. The door continued to open, and a band of peasants came pouring through.

"So, I assume there's a plan?" Jared asked.

Chapter 32
The Rescue Mission

Accompanied by the guards, Malum dragged Iyon down the steps leading to the deepest part of the dungeon. As they passed other cells, Iyon heard people weeping behind the barricaded doors. Anger rose up inside him, but, inhibited by the mask and chains, he was unable to do anything for them.

They entered a large room that contained what looked like a giant white mucous membrane with no visible door leading into or out of it. Tubes ran from the outer wall of this unique cell to a huge apparatus monitored by three soldiers. Malum motioned to a guard who pressed buttons and pushed levers, causing the cell wall to slowly slide apart, making an opening big enough for Malum to haul Iyon into his new home. Two guards followed them inside the cell where three white metallic poles formed a triangle. Malum dragged Iyon to the center of the triangle. The guards removed the chains from Malum's harness and clasped them onto the poles. As soon as the chains touched the poles and were locked into place, they converted to a white liquid metal.

Two heavy chains lay at the bottom of two of the poles, and the guards clasped them to Iyon's mask. These chains also turned to liquid metal, as well as the mask itself. Iyon groaned and fought against the chains as he immediately felt a draining of his power.

After the guards left, Malum gloated over his prized prisoner. He bent down to Iyon and snorted in his ear. "You've no idea what these chains can do to a being like you, Iyon. It will be impossible for you to ever escape, my friend, for this is a Warrior Horse's prison that I had carefully constructed, especially for you. I too was once trapped in one similar to this. You will lose all of yourself. Then Celesta can make you into whatever she desires. There is no way for you to beat this. A just revenge for what I had to endure. When it's all over, I will tell you who I am, but not until then."

Malum started to walk toward the exit, then glanced back at the golden collar around Iyon and the gem that was proudly positioned in the center of the chest plate. With all the strength within the dark horse, he exploded with power from his eyes and viciously attacked the collar, attempting to break it off of Iyon. To his great dismay, when he was done, the collar remained unscathed around him. Malum grunted in disgust. Iyon remained silent during the attack, hoping another would not come.

"When your power is drained, perhaps I will demand your beheading instead. I will have that breast plate for myself. It will be my greatest trophy."

Malum walked toward the exit, leaving Iyon to wonder who this mystery horse was.

"Close the cell wall, soldier," Malum ordered.

The cell wall slid shut, sealing Iyon inside.

....

Celesta strutted around her library and gazed triumphantly at her stolen treasures. The power and wealth she had gained so quickly made her feel invincible. After a few moments, she turned her attention back to Jen.

"I don't think Felonious wants the chest unlocked. I believe he wants the key, the chest, and the Key Holders destroyed. He already has your father trapped in an awful dungeon, probably being tortured in the most unimaginable way. Too bad his only rescuer won't be able to come to his aid."

Jen listened in horror to the words of this wicked queen.

"Well, that's enough playing around. It's time for you to get me that chest. Walk to the globe and open it up," Celesta ordered.

The queen smiled devilishly as she followed Jen to the hidden portal.

"Go now and find me that chest. You will pick it up, bring it back through the gateway, and place it at my feet. Go."

At Celesta's command, the vine put Jen's body into motion. Jen journeyed through the portal and began walking. She sensed that something was drawing her in a certain direction. It was powerful, like nothing she'd ever felt before. Jen wished she could resist, but found it utterly impossible to do so.

....

"A plan?" Rozor said. "We only have a map and a letter from Zurina, telling us to come to the castle when the doves are released. As soon as we saw the doves, we armed ourselves with the weapons we were able to hide from the queen and hurried here."

"What happened to your other weapons? I see only swords and pitch forks here."

"Not too long ago, the queen ended the famine in our city, so we didn't think she would ever hurt us. When Zurina confided in me that the queen was evil, I'll admit I was hesitant to believe her. But then I began to see things for myself. The guards in the city were replaced with more controlling ones who confiscated many of our weapons, all in the name of peace. Truth is, we're fighting against insurmountable odds, especially since the queen now practices black magic. We were reluctant to come until Zurina told us that others who have enough power to stand up to the queen would help us. The day I saw the great Warrior Horse, I knew that help had arrived. That's what encouraged us to come here when we saw the sign of the doves."

Jared tilted his head down and smiled, realizing that Zurina had taken a big risk in assuming he would actually show up. He looked up at Rozor, who was waiting for his response. "So Zurina's plan to overthrow the queen depends on us?"

Rozor said, "Yes, it does. Well, and the Warrior Horse she said would do most of the work." Then, knowing that he needed to share important information with Jared and Taq, Rozor briefly told the story of how they first found out about the queen's secret plans and tunnels.

"Zurina sent a revised map of the castle to the village architect after the queen redesigned the underground tunnels. Knowing that Kerch, our resident architect, would carefully study every inch of the map, Zurina wrote a cryptic message in the lower right-hand corner, instructing Kerch to flip it over. Since there was nothing there, he took a candle closer to it and then it revealed a message.

Rozor pulled out the parchment. Another townsman took his small lantern, opened the top, and placed it underneath. The heat from the candle inside revealed the message from Zurina. Rozor was about to read it but Jared put his hand over the parchment and stopped him short.

"Zurina did mention to hurry, so I trust the story. Let's have a look at that map, okay?"

"Of course, of course." After Rozor showed Jared the map, he pointed to the tunnels on it. "Queen Miriam had these hidden tunnels built under the corridors of the castle. They'll lead us to a narrow section called Rabbit's Hollow, which we can crawl through in order to get to what had been Queen Angelina's secret storage room. From there, we can infiltrate the castle."

Jared spoke up. "I'll take the lead, and Taq will bring up the rear. We'll advance until we find Jen. Iyon is here and is more than capable of handling that evil queen."

The men nodded their heads in agreement. They knew exactly what they were fighting for.

Jared was amazed by Zurina's hard work and impressed by her ingenious plan to defeat the queen. He now regretted ever doubting her. However, she played an incredible risky game assuming that he would even be there....

"Well," Jared said, "It sounds like Zurina has given us our best option." The group agreed and followed Rozor and Jared into Rabbit's Hollow.

Chapter 33
The Near Death, the Journey,
and the Transformation

Iyon lay on the ground in the cell in absolute silence. He concentrated on letting his breathing slow down. He knew these ancient chains had the ability to drain all the energy and power from their prisoner. The more a prisoner struggled to escape, the weaker he would get and the stronger the chains would become.

As Iyon continued his slow breathing pattern, his pulse almost stopped. Then the gem on his collar came to life as he willingly surrendered his power to it instead of the chains. At first, the gem was only a flickering light with the strength of a small candle, but then it gradually grew stronger and stronger. No one, not even the chains themselves, could detect the transformation taking place within Iyon and the sacred gem.

....

The golden sun remained steadfast while scattered cotton ball clouds drifted across the pale blue sky. The wind gently caressed Jen's face as she crossed the field. The atmosphere reminded her of her own world. How she wished she had the freedom to run through this field and pretend for just one moment that she was back home. A single tear rolled down her cheek. She tried to wipe it away, but the vine yanked her hand back down. All Jen could do was obey the queen's order to retrieve the chest. She felt like a marionette whose strings were being pulled by a sadistic madwoman.

Jen inhaled deeply and screamed, "Iyon! Where are...." She was cut short and gasped for breath as the vine tightened around her neck. It held its grip until Jen thought she would pass out. Finally, it loosened. Jen groaned as she was forced to continue the journey.

The vine could control her body, but it could not control her thoughts. How could Iyon walk so easily into a trap and let himself be captured? What's happened to him? Is he even still alive?

Iyon, can you hear me? I hope you're okay. I need your help. Find me, Iyon. Find me.

....

Queen Celesta stood at the entrance of the portal, watching her magic vine and Jen as they started their journey. With the vine gone, this was Zurina's only chance. Since she was already standing, she turned toward the fruit platter and, taking the vial from the folds of her dress, she surreptitiously poured it over the grapes which immediately soaked up the elixir, leaving no remnant of the elixir behind.

"Zurina," the queen called while still gazing into the globe.

Zurina placed the vial back in her pocket, then lifted the platter and said, "Hungry, Mistress?"

Celesta strolled over to her chair and sat down. "I suppose."

"Here's your favorite. These were grown special and have an extra bite to them."

Celesta reached down, picked up a small bunch of grapes and ate them.

"Mmm, these are extraordinary." She stuffed several more in her mouth, unable to resist the flavor. Talking with her mouth full, she said, "Soon that girl will return with my chest. Yes, things are definitely working in my favor."

....

The freedom fighters were making their way through Rabbit's Hollow, which barely had enough space for a grown man to crawl.

"Was anybody considering how a man would fit through here when this was being built?" complained one of the peasants. "Now I know why they call it Rabbit's Hollow. Ouch! Jared, you stepped on my fingers."

"Quit your grumbling," called Rozor from the front. "We're almost there." Rozor crawled a few more feet and turned a sharp corner. "We've made it to the end. I see the opening, but it's covered by a grate. I'll try to punch it out." Once Rozor reached the grate, he punched at the bars with all his might, but they wouldn't budge.

"Rozor, allow me," Jared called from behind. He pulled his laser gun from his side. With one blast, the grate was completely vaporized.

Rozor's head poked out of the small hole, and he took a quick look around. The next passageway was much larger. Light came from a castle room to the left. Rozor crawled out of the hole on his belly until he was able to get his feet.

"The entrance to Queen Angelina's storage room is straight ahead. Come on, men, let's move."

....

Jen reached the end of the field lined with trees that looked like weeping willows. A babbling brook wound its way to a waterfall that echoed in the distance. A powerful unseen energy continued to pull her upstream. The vine gave way a little, letting this other supernatural entity guide her.

Jen continued on her journey until she reached a small shallow pool of water at the base of a forty-foot waterfall. She could tell right away that this was no ordinary waterfall. The water cascading over the cliff looked like an impenetrable wall. Surprisingly, no waves or splashes were made when the water hit the pool.

Pulled onward by the entity, Jen was drawn into the water where she saw another astounding sight. There, standing in the pool, calmly getting a drink, was Iyon! He had appeared out of nowhere. To Jen's surprise, the vine had no reaction to her seeing him. She tried to whisper his name, but the vine choked her.

Iyon stopped drinking and looked up at Jen. He didn't move his mouth, but spoke to her telepathically.

The vine isn't aware of me, for I'm an illusion and only you can see me. I heard your cry, and so I found you. Don't be afraid, Jen. I'll be with you shortly, and soon this will all be over. You must trust me. As soon as you're given a chance to open the chest, you must do so immediately.

You must open it alone because if Celesta opens it along with you, then all that's pure and good inside the chest will be corrupted.

By the time he finished communicating with Jen, she'd reached the wall of water. Peering directly into it, she could see that it was moving at such an incredible speed, it seemed to be standing still, so that she could see her reflection as if looking into a mirror.

How can I possibly pass through this? It's going to kill me for sure! Holding her breath, Jen closed her eyes and felt herself being pulled into the falls. As she entered the wall of water, it pulled apart in almost the exact shape of her body. When Jen opened her eyes, she was on the other side, facing a cavern made of pure quartz. The entire room glistened as if she were standing inside a diamond. Directly in front of her was a staircase made of diamonds. The vine guided her up the steps until she reached the top, giving her a view of the entire cave. Glancing at the back of the cave, Jen saw a quartz table holding a chest. To the right of the table was a gaunt elderly man lying on a bed of feathers. He wore a faded plaid shirt and overalls. A carpenter's belt was hooked around his waist with pockets for wrenches, hammers, and other important tools. A leather bound journal lay next to him on the featherbed. She walked up to get a better look at him. His skin was wrinkled and caved in against his bones and he was breathing ever so slowly.

"Hello," she said tenderly.

He didn't open his eyes. He moved his lips so slightly that his words were barely audible.

"Key Holder, you've come at last. Now I can have my rest. So long I have hidden, so long I have waited. Take care…of…the…power…inside." He breathed his last and was gone. She couldn't even get his name.

She stared down at him for one more moment, but the vine grew impatient and pushed her hands into action. She tried to go for his journal, curious what wonders it must have possessed, but instead, she was only allowed to clasp the handles of the chest and lift it off the table. The vine compelled her to leave the old man's side and directed her down the steps and back toward the wall of water. Her heart was filled with sadness at having encountered death so suddenly. The feeling of a sudden emptiness of a man she never knew left her bereft and full of sorrow, as if she had known him her whole life.

Jen left her eyes open as she hit the glass-like wall of water. Although the water poured down all around her with an overbearing force, not one drop touched her, or the chest, or the vine wrapped so tightly around her. After passing through the waterfall, Jen looked frantically for Iyon, but his image had already faded away. She was physically exhausted. Trudging out of the water, she longed to lie down and rest, but when she attempted to do so, the merciless vine jerked her to her feet and forced her to carry the chest back through the field. With every step came the dread of having to face Celesta and a life of servitude. The anxiety was killing Jen. She struggled to regain her strength as she let Iyon's words play over and over in her mind. You must trust me…you must trust me. Jen clung on to that; it was all she had left to cling on to.

....

The men crowded into the storage room. Dust and cobwebs covered everything. Taq was the first to notice something hanging from the ceiling.

"Jared, look up!" Taq said nervously.

All the men became aware of a giant net that resembled a cobweb made of dark metal.

"Blast it!" Jared yelled.

Malum had been hiding in the corridor, waiting. As soon as he heard blasting, he bolted into the room through the wall-like arched doorway. With power from his eyes, he sliced the chain holding the net and it fell on top of the men. They did their best to lift it in an effort to escape, but the net was full of dark magic. Instantly, the dark metal net separated into little strands that bent and wrapped themselves around the men's hands, binding them behind their backs. The strands also bound their feet together as well, causing the men to squirm helplessly on the ground. Within minutes, Malum captured all of them. No one escaped.

"Guards!" the great black beast bellowed.

Several foot soldiers ran into the room and surrounded the pile of men that totaled fifty in all.

"I told you I smelled venom in my lair. That's why I set traps throughout the castle. Gag these traitors of the queen and drag them to the interrogation cells." Malum walked around the pile of captured men and looked for one specifically. As soon as he found him, Malum used his mighty hoof to kick the fallen soldier away from the others, slamming him against the wall. Malum snapped his front leg up and pressed it against Jared, keeping him up against the stone wall and then glared into his face with an expression of utter hatred.

"It's been a long time, Jared. I'll enjoy watching your execution, but not until you have been punished and tortured for days on end. I will see to it that it is as unbearable as it can be. And Iyon won't be coming to your rescue. I was once trapped in a cell built for Warrior Horses. And now, he is in one! Escape will be impossible." He said to the guards, "Make sure this one goes in a private cell. String him up and beat him as hard as you like, but make sure he doesn't die before I get to him."

Jared stared into the horse's eyes and saw nothing but a deep hatred and contempt, full of a blood-thirsty revenge for him. His mind raced through memories to see if there was ever a time he had wronged such a beast, but no such occurrence came to mind.

Two burly soldiers seized Jared. One of them, seeing Jared's weapon lying on the floor, picked it up and kept it for himself. "You won't need this anymore," he scoffed, and dragged Jared out of the room.

Rozor tried to warn the soldiers before his mouth was bound shut. "Wait— you don't understand, the queen, she's really a wi-..." He couldn't get the full word out. Others tried to speak, but the armed guards were too fast.

Malum gave one last order. "Check the corridor they came through.

Make sure no other rebels are sneaking around. And when you take these prisoners to the cell room, string them all up and start flogging them."

Malum scowled at the sorry pack of men lying all over the ground. "The rest of you will be executed in the public square by noon tomorrow. And if you think your Iyon will be rescuing you, think again. He's my prisoner as well," Malum snorted, smoke pouring from his nostrils. And with that, he exited the room.

....

Iyon knew that he had successfully reached Jen. Now it was time. During the past few hours, he had been surrendering all his power to the gem in his collar so that he himself would be an empty vessel. Through this transfer of power, the gem's brilliance increased in intensity until it shone brighter than the sun. Iyon's eyes remained closed beneath the liquid mask and his breathing was at a standstill. Iyon's heart stopped as he knew he must surrender everything. And then he died. The poles and chains searched throughout the dead being, hungrily looking for the power to suck but finding nothing. They glowed in a dead white, angry for not finding any more power, for all it knew and all it had been created for was to take life and energy.

That is when the magic happened; for so mysterious and wonderful are the transformations that can come from death—the greatest sacrifice and the greatest new beginning. The gem began shaking in its collar from all the power within it. It was as if Iyon's entire being, power, and soul was captured within the gem and now intermingled with the untold mysteries that extend from the beginning of time to its very end. The great transformation completed.

Light shot out from the gem like rays of glowing white metal. It slashed away at Iyon's chains, causing them to fall to pieces and disintegrate to powder. The poles withered and died as the power was taken back from them. The mask was cut in two and fell from Iyon's face, breaking into thousands of tiny particles. The gem infused Iyon with all its power. Now, standing majestically and glowing like a white-golden statue, he readied himself to take on the dark horse and bring down Celesta.

164

Chapter 34
Light and Darkness Collide

Completely exhausted after carrying the chest across the field, Jen finally made it to the portal. Once through, she proceeded to the queen and placed the chest at her feet.

"Now the time has come! Key Holder, take the key and unlock the chest." Jen's body was forced to obey. She whimpered as her hand reached for the key, but then stopped abruptly. The queen looked puzzled.

"I said, unlock the chest!" But the vine paid her no heed. Instead, it thrust Jen over to the table where Zurina had placed the grapes and began sucking them as it desired its elixir. Realizing that the grapes had been tainted with the elixir, an enraged Celesta stood up and glared at Zurina.

"You traitor! What did you do to those grapes?"

"It wasn't me, Mistress. I swear!"

Furious, Celesta raised her hands and, using her black magic, lifted Zurina in the air and threw her against the wall. As soon as she hit the wall, cuffs formed around her hands, feet, and neck, holding her fast.

Out of anger and desperation, Zurina yelled out to Celesta, "Please! Stop now before it's too late!"

"Shut up, you traitor! To think that I actually trusted you! I won't make that mistake again.

"Celesta, I didn't poison the grapes!" Zurina lied in hopes to preserve her life just a few more minutes.

Celesta could no longer stand to listen to her, so she had the wall wrap itself around Zurina's mouth. Taking a few steps toward her, Celesta sneered, "You're such a fool! When this is all over you will be forced to tell the truth. All I can say for you is if you thought those two months were misery, well, just wait! That will look like freedom compared to what I'm going to do to you next!"

Just then Malum entered. "Celesta," he snorted, "I discovered a small band of rebels breaking into the castle, but they were easily captured. They've been taken to the dungeon for flogging."

"Good. Now go check on Iyon. I want that horse's power drained so I can transfer it to myself. I don't want any more setbacks!"

"Do you want that one taken to the dungeon?" Malum asked, motioning his head toward Zurina.

"No, I want her to witness my triumph. Then I plan to kill Jen before her eyes and cast a spell on her to force out the truth behind her betrayal."

Celesta stared in disgust as she realized that the elixir's power over the vine far exceeded hers. By now the vine had wrapped Jen's hands and feet together and held onto her while it gorged on the tainted grapes.

....

Rays sharper than a two-edged sword shot from Iyon's eyes and slashed through the cell membrane. Leaping through the opening, Iyon expected to find Malum with a multitude of guards. But instead, all he saw were three soldiers manning the machine that operated his cell. Their jaws dropped as they stared in shock at the radiant splendor of Iyon.

Iyon sliced the machine in two with his powerful tail. Blue rays shot out from his eyes, knocking the men to the ground. Then with the newfound power, Iyon transformed his blue rays into cords that wrapped around the soldiers. Raising the men in the air, he carried them to the next cell, dropped them to the ground, and kicked the door closed behind him. When another guard came around the corner, Iyon shot out a blue ray that coiled around the soldier's chest with an iron grip. He pulled the soldier to himself, threw him in a cell and, with the whip of his tail, closed and locked the door.

Iyon proceeded up the corridor. On his way out of the dungeon, he passed a triple-thick iron door. It was locked from the inside. With one kick, the door broke down and he entered the room and witnessed an appalling sight. Fifty men were hanging from the ceiling by chains, and the soldiers were laughing maliciously with delight as they mocked the prisoners on how they would be beaten. Some of the prisoners were already being punched and kicked.

All laughing stopped when the guards caught sight of the Warrior Horse standing in the doorway. In seconds, the room was covered with a sheet of blue energy that radiated from Iyon. The chains holding the men disintegrated and then the blue energy turned into glowing chains and wrapped around all of the soldiers and bound their hands and feet together.

"Confiscate the weapons of the queen's soldiers," Iyon commanded.

As soon as Rozor was freed, he called out to Iyon, "If you know a man named Jared, he's here also. The black horse had him taken to a different prison cell."

"Jared?" said Iyon. "He came by himself?"

"No, there was another...."

"He came with me," called Taq. Iyon hadn't noticed him, for he had been hanging in the center, surrounded by other men.

"Where's your weapon?" Iyon demanded.

"It was destroyed."

Iyon pricked his ears back and listened intently for even the slightest groan made by Jared.

Suddenly, Iyon's ears flattened and his eyes darkened. He turned to his left and shot out blue power, blasting a hole through the next three prison walls. He bounded through the openings and landed in a cell where Jared was being beaten.

Jared's hands were in chains from the ceiling and his feet were bound to the ground so that he could not move, and he was only wearing his loin cloth. The guards were circling Jared with metal-like whips and smoldering brands, whipping him and branding him wherever they pleased. They were quickly bound hand and foot with Iyon's coils and he threw them to the far corner of the cell. Iyon's heart pounded in pain and anger at having not gotten there sooner for his friend as they had already covered the upper half of Jared's body with gashes and brand marks that were still smoking. Iyon pressed against his bloody body with his golden face and let the ancient power enter into his friend. The ancient power came like a river and began healing Jared. The gashes closed and the smoldering of the brands faded as new skin formed over it. Jared screamed and he shook, overwhelmed at the sensation of instant healing across his entire body. After Iyon was finished, he cut his friend down carefully to make sure that he was able to land on his feet.

Jared panted from the transformation that just took place in him. He grabbed Iyon and hugged him tight as he fought to catch his breath. "Thank you, my friend."

Jared walked over to the guards who were lying on the ground, reached inside the armor of the one who'd previously confiscated his laser gun. "Well, I guess I will need this after all!" Jared said as he took back his weapon, and grabbed his shirt and pants that had been thrown to the corner when they were stringing him up.

"Meet me upstairs," Iyon said.

He closed his eyes, reached deep inside himself as he focused the new power, and sensed Jen's presence. "I'm going to get Jen. Malum will be here shortly. I can sense his coming presence, so hurry. Leave through the back."

Iyon didn't wait for a response. He vaporized holes through pure rock and then several floors of thick stone in the castle. He flew straight up. Jared leaped through the openings in the walls that led back to the other men. They had seized the weapons from the guards and ran through the back tunnels as Iyon had instructed, taking out anyone who stood in their path.

....

Malum trotted confidently into the dungeon, expecting to find Iyon half dead. But instead, to his great dismay, he discovered that the cell wall was torn in two, and Iyon was nowhere in sight. Then, turning toward the great machine, he found that it also had been cut in two and its lines severed, sparking and sizzling in shameful defeat.

"Iyon!" the black beast roared. He galloped down a corridor, only to find the queen's guards wrapped in glowing coils and calling for mercy.

"You incompetent fools!" Malum yelled.

His angry eyes, blazing like a raging fire, shot out rays to annihilate them. But the strength of Iyon's coils protected them. Seething, Malum galloped out of the dungeon and headed back to the library in order to confront his hated enemy. On his way out, he decided he would first kill Jared, or so he thought.

....

The band of peasants, led by Jared and Rozor, made their way through the tunnels, fighting with the weapons they'd confiscated from the captured guards. They advanced as an unstoppable united force until they reached the hallway that led to the queen's library, which was filled with armed guards.

Jared called out to the fifty men behind him, "Fight for the freedom of your families! It's time to take back this kingdom from the witch who enslaved it!"

The men let out a battle cry and stormed through the entrance. The desire for freedom became their source of strength. They jumped, pounced, slashed, and blasted, determined to defeat the enemy at any cost, as they made their way closer to Jen. There was nothing that could stop the stamina and determination of this small band of mighty men.

....

After the queen threatened to deny the disobedient vine the elixir ever again, the creature reluctantly stopped eating the grapes and dragged Jen back to the chest.

Then, speaking to the vine, Celesta said, "Only allow her to turn the key. Then I'll open the chest so that all of its power will be mine."

Celesta was now standing directly behind Jen. With trembling fingers, Jen put the key into the lock. When it turned, thunder rumbled from inside the chest. Celesta grabbed Jen and shoved her to the side. The floor near one end of the room exploded, hurling debris and stones everywhere. Iyon flew through the hole and landed ten yards from Jen and Queen Celesta.

His whole body blazed like melted gold. He immediately shot a ray at Celesta, causing her to jump back away from the chest. Fuming, Celesta glared at this stallion who dared to get in the way of her plans.

Fearful that Jen would open the chest, Celesta hissed, "Vine, don't let that girl touch the chest!" The vine obeyed, but very reluctantly, because the scent of the elixir on the remaining grapes was so enticing.

With her hands and feet now bound together, Jen lay on the floor next to the chest, frustrated that she couldn't get to it. The vine sniffed the ground and the air, becoming more agitated. Seeing that the queen was preoccupied with Iyon, the vine slithered over to the remaining grapes, dragging Jen along behind it.

"Time for you to die, horse!" Celesta raised her arms in the air and, using her black magic, formed a ball of electrifying energy between her hands. The light from the sphere danced with the reflection of the gems on her gown.

She hurled the ball at Iyon. He saw it heading straight for him, but he didn't move. Celesta laughed sadistically as the ball of energy hit Iyon directly in the chest and exploded. When the light cleared, Celesta's laughter stopped as she saw Iyon standing there, untouched and unharmed. She snarled as she saw how useless her attack was on him. In desperation, she created three more energy balls. Before releasing them, she tried to distract Iyon by yelling, "Vine! Kill the girl!" She knew it would only take a second for the vine to snap Jen's neck. While charging across the room to rescue Jen, Iyon emitted his own powerful blue rays from his eyes that cut through the three energy balls as if they were thin paper, and destroyed them. "You'll never get to her in time!" Celesta sneered, smiling maliciously. She turned toward Jen, expecting the girl to be dead, but her smile vanished when she saw that Jen was still alive. The vine was so busy devouring the grapes with the intoxicating elixir that it had completely ignored Celesta's orders.

Outraged, the queen looked at Zurina, who was struggling to break from the wall. Celesta threw a metallic ball of energy with a spell of death on it, but Iyon intercepted it. Then he sliced away at Zurina's cuffs, and she fell to the ground.

Malum flew up through the hole and landed next to the queen. Iyon was caught by surprise last time, but not this time, and so Iyon attacked them both. While rays from the gem blasted the black beast, beams from Iyon's eyes assailed the queen. His power propelled them both through the back wall and into the next room.

Malum was shocked by the level of strength Iyon now displayed. He looked angrily at the queen, who was struggling to pull herself out of the debris.

"Your plans are failing! What use are you to me?" the black horse snarled.

Leaping over the wreckage, Iyon faced Malum and Celesta.

The vine slashed like a whip at Zurina as she ran toward Jen.

Malum noticed Zurina going to Jen's aid. Knowing that Jen had to be prevented from opening the chest, he darted to the left and managed to get a shot past Iyon. Zurina saw the blast heading straight for Jen and jumped in front of the deadly ray. The blast struck her in the shoulder, flipping her in the air. Her body crashed to the floor. She lay there, motionless.

Jen screamed in terror. Her mind raced as she tried to think of a way to free herself from the vine. Suddenly, she felt the vine loosening its hold on her. Having eaten all the grapes filled with the elixir, the intoxicated vine could still smell more. It released Jen and slithered off, frantically following the aroma.

Seeing that the vine had set her free, Malum and Celesta leaped far above Iyon, sending out blasts at both him and the girl, trying in every way to destroy Jen before she could open the chest. Suddenly, the gem around Iyon's chest created a yellow wall of light that shot straight up to the ceiling in a fraction of a second. Malum and the queen slammed into it and fell to the ground.

Jen lunged for the chest, put her hands on the lid, and opened it.

Celesta screamed in horror as she watched. Seeing that the battle was lost, Malum pulled himself up and fled while everyone else was distracted.

The vine, which had caught the scent of the elixir on the queen's breath, flew straight to her, binding her hands, feet, and neck. Then one strand of the vine held her mouth open while another one slid down her throat in search of its favorite food. Celesta tried to fight back, but it was useless. The vine bound her so tightly that she lost her balance and flopped clumsily to the ground.

Out of the chest flowed a river of light. It rose like a mighty wave, encircling Jen until she could no longer be seen.

Jared and the others stormed the room, ready for battle, but stopped and marveled when they saw the river of light dancing with Jen in the air that lasted for several minutes. Her countenance glowed as she was slowly lowered to the ground and the radiant river returned to the chest and the lid closed by itself. Its work with her was complete, for now.

She turned and saw Zurina lying among the shattered pieces of the wall. Jen went to her. Bending down, she placed her hands on the broken body. A portion of the light from the chest flowed out of Jen's hands and infused Zurina, healing her. The young woman opened her eyes. Looking up, she saw a light around a familiar face and smiled.

The queen lay on the ground next to Iyon. The vine had wrapped around her body and gagged her, preventing her from casting any spells.

When the peasants noticed that the queen was indeed defeated, they shouted and jumped for joy. The battle was over. They were finally free.

Chapter 35
Homeward Bound

Iyon and Jen wasted no time going from cell to cell. He broke down the prison doors, and she laid hands on those who were injured, healing them. When they came to the lowest region of the dungeon, they found Sidian, who was tightly bound in chains and hanging from the ceiling.

"We know that you are not a true follower of the queen. When you saw a chance to thwart her plans, you risked your life to try to stop her. Therefore, we release you. You're free to go," they said as they unchained him.

"Thank you for judging me fairly. From this day forward, I'll do what I can to make Eshron a great city again."

Then Iyon moved on to other sections of the castle. Using the power of the gem, he put fallen pillars upright and restored the walls and floors to their original state. After a thorough search, Celesta's spell books were discovered and burned. All evil was purged from the castle.

Jared and Rozor left their men rounding up Celesta's soldiers. In hopes of getting leniency, those who'd sided with the queen confessed that they'd stolen goods and many precious artifacts from other worlds. It was decided that their punishment was to return the goods to the various worlds and hand the thieves over to those worlds for judgment. Two of the captured soldiers led Iyon, Jen, and Rozor down to the secret cavern that held Tor. When they arrived at the site, the stalactites and stalagmites that had kept the vortex in place had been destroyed. Tor was gone. Iyon glared at the wreckage that was undoubtedly the work of Malum. Iyon knew he hadn't seen the last of him.

The vine was also gone. After it had released Celesta, it had escaped into the forest.

Gagged and heavily wrapped in coils produced by Iyon, Celesta sat in a small caged wagon, awaiting her punishment.

Because of the queen's knowledge of black magic, the people of Eshron feared that they didn't have a jail cell strong enough to hold her. To make sure Celesta would never escape, Iyon told the people that he had planned to take her with him and imprison her in Tranquil Earth under the watchful eye of Hope.

In recognition of his leadership in the rebellion against the evil queen, Rozor was unanimously chosen to be the new king of Eshron. He and his people were in the field outside the castle walls, saying farewell to the departing warriors and freed prisoners from Tranquil Earth. The sun was shining bright that day, as if celebrating with them and the eastern winds swept peacefully across the land.

Jen, Iyon, Jared, and Zurina stood together, basking in the warmth of the sun and the joy of victory. Jen, dressed in a white sari given to her by the grateful people of Eshron, stood on Iyon's right side, stroking his mane. By now Iyon was no longer glowing gold. He relinquished much of the power back into the gem in order to be kept safe for another day. To his left were Jared and Zurina, her long dark hair cascading past her shoulders instead of having it pulled back as she normally did.

Rozor looked at them with eyes that expressed indescribable appreciation. "Thank you for freeing us from that treacherous witch and her evil plot to enslave us all." Then, directing his attention to the Zurina, he continued, "My dear, you have endured so much, at times seeing no light or hope of any kind. Your strength and determination have inspired all of us here in Eshron. Your faithfulness will never be forgotten."

Zurina responded, "Thank you for choosing to believe in me even when my actions made me seem untrustworthy. Rest assured that Celesta will get her due punishment."

The new king nodded his head. Celesta turned away in disgust.

"It's time for us to go," Iyon pronounced.

Jen mounted Iyon. She held out her hands, and the River Chest floated directly to her. She opened the chest only a crack, letting out an incredibly bright stream of light. All the people around had to turn their heads and cover their eyes, but not Jen. Her eyes stayed steadfast as the river of light formed a large portal right there in the field. As soon as the opening was large enough for them to travel through, the light flowed back into the chest. Jen closed the lid and locked it with the key.

As Iyon walked toward the portal, the gem on his collar began to glow, causing the caged wagon holding Celesta to follow him. Celesta glared contemptuously at Eshron's new king as she disappeared into the portal. Jared and Zurina went next, leading all the freed captives from Tranquil Earth. The people of Eshron cheered and waved good-bye as the swirling mass shrank into itself until it was no more.

Chapter 36
The Beginning of the End

The people of Tolare witnessed an anomaly of blazing white in the valley and feared they were being invaded. Some started running frantically for cover. Others stood steadfast, fascinated by the brilliant light. Those who stayed were pleasantly surprised when they saw, emerging from the radiance, Jen and Iyon with Jared and Zurina. Behind them were hundreds of refugees, who were thought had been killed by the Skeign.

Hope declared a national week of thanksgiving. An immense celebration, which included feasting and dancing, took place in Tolare in honor of all those returning from Pure Earth. Even Dahlia, who rarely ventured beyond the boundary of her garden, came to rejoice with everyone.

Jasmin and her many friends, dressed in pastel-colored dresses and with garlands of flowers on their heads, danced about the streets, along with many others.

On the first day of the celebration, Iyon wandered through the crowd, searching for Jen, but couldn't find her there. Looking up at the temple, he sensed she was waiting for him. Iyon trotted up the stone path that led to the temple. He slowed down and stepped off the path so he wouldn't make any noise. When he got close to the pillars, he peered through the bushes surrounding them. There was Jen, standing near the edge of the circle in the temple. She was dressed in a military uniform that was fashioned especially for women warriors. Her shoulders were pushed back, and her hands were clasped behind her. She was no longer the timid, defeated young girl that first came here, but a warrior.

"You can come out of the bushes, Iyon. I know it's you," Jen said, happy that he was there.

Iyon snorted a little, and walked into the center of the stone circle.

Jen turned and stared into his eyes, raised her hand and stroked his forehead.

"Will you be coming with me, Iyon, or do you plan on missing all the action?"

It hadn't even been a full twelve hours since their return, and Jen was ready to leave. Iyon didn't want to admit it, but he had become very proud of who she had become.

"I will be joining you," he said with determination of a sure victory in his tone.

"We have the ability to rescue him now. It's time to find my father."

"They may be expecting us," he warned.

"Or maybe not. It's only been a half a day. Chances are word has not gotten to them yet."

Challenging her determination, Iyon added, "When he does find out, Felonious will undoubtedly wage war against us. Are you ready for that?"

"I'll face whatever or whomever I have to in order to get my father back. And then together we'll find my mother."

"Then you're ready. Let's go."

Jen smiled at her trusted friend. Iyon struck the center of the temple floor. It lowered and the two vanished.

Chapter 37

A Message from the Darkness
to the Worlds of Earth

After the Master received the dreadful news of the opening of the River Chest, he cried out and cursed all the worlds of Earth and everyone else who would dare oppose him.

"Humans and all who try to resist me: I'm coming for you. I'm coming for all of you. You think you can defeat me, but you're wrong. Don't think for a second you'll be ready for me, for I'll come as your best friend, your neighbor, or someone you think you can trust. In the midst of my lies, there you will be, accepting me, wanting me, needing me, and being deceived into believing you can't live without me. I will destroy every one of you, and you pathetic, unsuspecting fools will be praising my name as I do it."

The dark regions where the Master thrived bellowed with his war cry.

"My time is now!"